LOOK FOR LUCA

J.W.DARCY

JASMINE BRITE MYSTERIES No.1

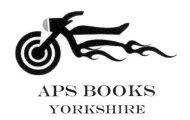

APS BOOKS
YORKSHIRE

APS Books,
The Stables, Field Lane,
Aberford,
West Yorkshire,
LS25 3AE

APS Books is a subsidiary of
the APS Publications imprint

www.andrewsparke.com

First published 2018

For my wonderful family, who always believed this could happen and Zsanett Kuti for her patience and support.

Thank you all.

PROLOGUE
9th May 1978 Milan, Italy

THE hot, humid air was suffocating and Kate struggled to remain upright in the over-crowded Metro carriage.

Luca was restless in her arms, sensing the taut atmosphere around him, just as Kate could. Something was going on, that was evident. The normally relaxed, short daily commute into the centre had suddenly been swamped with excitable young Italians, all loudly discussing something that, unfortunately, her understanding of Italian wasn't up to yet. Whatever it was, they all seemed to be heading for the same place she needed to be.

Was it the Duomo they were all making for? The vast Cathedral stood in its magnificence, right in the heart of Milan's famous designer shopping district. Its Piazza was filled with nearly as many pigeons as visitors and was a place to sit and just watch the world go by.

As she was roughly ejected out of the doors and carried along with the crowd, Luca began to cry in alarm.

"Don't worry, Caro, we'll be outside in a moment," she comforted the toddler.

Barely eighteen months old, Luca was her sole charge and the means to her living and working in Milan for her gap year. It was a way of learning the Italian language and also travelling whilst under the protection of her wealthy employers, Marcello and Francesca Buscolli. As their child-minder, she led a lifestyle that was popular with many English girls and the families gained bi-lingual children, on the cheap. She had been here for nearly eight months and loved her new life. She had come to love Luca almost as much as his mother did, possibly more so, it sometimes felt like to her. She would never understand how the wealthy seemed to have no desire to spend time with their children, except as something to be admired by other friends but always on the periphery of their own busy lives.

As they emerged into the sunlight at street level, Kate could see that the whole of the square surrounding the Duomo, was crowded with ever more chanting students.

Turning to a passing woman who was hastily going in the opposite direction, Kate asked "Scusi, Signora che cosa sta accendo?"

1

"La Presidente, il mort!" the woman shouted. Then realising that Kate was not Italian, she said it again this time in English; "President Aldo Moro is dead. He 'as been found in the boot of a car in Rome. Do not stay here with the child, Signorina. It not safe. They protest against the government and Il Brigate Rosse. It not safe. Go home!"

With that, she rushed off, seemingly eager to be away from the angry mob. Kate stood watching, unsure of what to do now. The sensible thing to do was follow the woman's advice. Luca was struggling and beginning to cry in her arms. He wanted to get down and explore as usual and to chase the pigeons that constantly battled for space with the humans in the square but there was nowhere to put him down safely. The shops were pulling down their shutters and closing in anticipation of trouble.

However, Kate was supposed to be meeting Raphael. She had no means of contacting her boyfriend as they always met here on the steps of the Duomo. Telephone conversations were too awkward for them as each had little command of the other's language beyond basic conversation. The family did not know that she met him while she had their son in her charge. She knew that they would be angry but they allowed her so little free time to herself she felt that she had no option. Besides, Raphael adored Luca and spent much of their time together playing with the boy. She had no worries on that score and he was so attractive and amusing. She deserved some fun she reasoned and he had already won her heart. So much so that she couldn't see herself leaving Milan anytime soon.

As she was turning to make her way back towards the Metro station she spotted Raphael walking quickly towards her on the other side of the square. He was beckoning her with his arm and as he caught up with her he said, hurriedly, "Veni qui, Vite! Vite!"

He reached for her hand and quickly led her away from the angry, shocked crowd that continued to fill up the small square, their loud cries still ringing in her ear.

1
2008

RUSH hour traffic was not helping Jasmine Brite's mood.

The call from the office had taken her by surprise. It was late in the day and business had been quiet for months now. She had given her younger brother, Hugo, orders to spruce up the website and attract more interest or it would be curtains for the company and unemployment for them all.

Jasmine had run a fairly successful on-line Missing Persons agency since leaving university with a Masters in Criminal Investigation and Psychology. She had used money from a legacy left to herself and Hugo when their parents had died in a car crash ten years ago. Since then she had taken over the role of parent to her, then fourteen-year-old brother and was fiercely protective of him but he really needed a kick up the backside too frequently for her liking. She was a lively, go-getting high achiever and Hugo was – well - exceptionally good at sitting at his computer all day. That had turned out to be his saving grace, however. Her agency could not operate without his genius level expertise on the technology front.

As she took more cases on she had been able to increase her staff and now employed three people whom she also regarded as best friends. They had brought their own particular skills to the agency and for that, Jasmine paid them accordingly. All in all, the agency had been ticking away nicely but what she really needed was a good mystery to get her teeth into instead of the daily grind of finding errant husbands and wives who often simply did not want to be found. She realised this was a selfish attitude on her part. She didn't mean that she wanted to find a victim of foul play but it was so satisfying and life affirming to re-unite the lost with their families. If only someone could do the same for her and Hugo. Perhaps this was why she had chosen this profession, as for her, the pain would never go away.

It was Hugo who had called her mobile just as she was heading home early for the day. An e-mail had just come in from a potential client and he had thought it was worth setting up a meeting. So, Jasmine was now heading to a service station halfway between her Midlands home and London. She hoped this trip was going to be worth it. The client had written that it was a thirty years old case but very little else. However, she had heard good things about The Brite Agency and thought if anyone could help her it would be them.

Jasmine wondered where the recommendation had come from but was pleased it had and she would find out soon enough anyway.

Fifty minutes later she pulled into the crowded service station and began looking for a soft-topped silver BMW Cabriolet. Not too many of those around here, she mused. As she drew up alongside the car she felt her embarrassingly small second-hand Kia was insignificant looking next to it.

The two women acknowledged each other and Jasmine mouthed that she was The Brite Agency's representative. The woman nodded and proceeded to get out of her car. Jasmine, too, got out, they shook hands and agreed to go into the cafeteria and buy coffees and something to eat before getting down to business.

Soon they were sitting in a quiet corner and Jasmine said, "How can I be of help?"

The woman introduced herself as Santa Buscolli. "And I need help to discover what happened to my younger brother, Luca."

Jasmine might have guessed her nationality by the names, without hearing the faintly Italian inflection in Santa's voice. Her dark hair, brown eyes, olive skin and immaculate dress sense all screamed Mediterranean heritage - also money and class. Santa's voice had a pleasing, languid tone that was like melting chocolate to the ear.

"Ok, Santa. May I call you that?"

Santa nodded of course and smiled.

"When did your brother go missing, where from and how old was he at the time? Why are you searching now and are the police still involved in the case?" Jasmine shot off her opening questions in rapid succession.

"Well, firstly my parents, as of last month, are no longer alive. My mother has just passed away and sadly my father died many years ago."

Jasmine offered her condolences and let her continue.

"And as to my brother's disappearance and probable death, it occurred in 1978. He was eighteen months old. So, no one is looking for him anymore, certainly not the police. I know it is thirty years ago and I don't know if you would be prepared to take on such an old case but I am desperate to give it one last chance now that I have no family left. Mama refused to discuss it, but now she's gone I need to try again, one last time. Please, I have just a little hope that your agency may have the resources to look into this. Money is no object. I have more than I will ever need. He is my family and I must do this for him," she ended, lowering her head, forlornly.

Jasmine sat quietly taking in all the information that Santa had supplied. So, this was truly what was now commonly called a Cold Case. Something to get her teeth into, certainly, and all the better because the raw emotions that came along with a recently missing child had been dampened down many years ago, she hoped. It was always easier to gather information when the client was thinking rationally. On the other hand, thirty years was a hell of a long time to have to start digging up leads and any witnesses to the crime. She relished the idea, even so.

She took out her lap-top and proceeded to take down details from Santa Buscolli and labelled the file No. 68 – Looking for Luca. She told Santa, "I'd be delighted to take on the case," and that she hoped whatever else she uncovered, to be able to give her closure, that over-used, under-valued phrase embarrassingly tripping off her tongue.

Santa thanked her profusely and asked if Jasmine would be prepared to travel down to her family home in London so that they could discuss in detail the circumstances of Luca's disappearance in a more congenial setting. "I've got photos and information to give you a starting point for the task."

As Miss Buscolli had already stated she would pay for Jasmine's services upfront, Jasmine had no problem with that arrangement. They agreed to meet at the weekend - Santa had a city job in finance so she would be free then. She gave Jasmine her business card and Jasmine gave Santa hers with her mobile number printed on it.

They shook hands, Santa once again, thanking Jasmine for taking the case on and said goodbye.

Jasmine decided to stay on and have a meal before making the journey home but Santa had declined to join her, saying she wasn't hungry.

Even lacking essential details, Jasmine could feel the familiar buzz of excitement in her stomach that she got when she was on the trail of a missing person. It was what made this job the best in the world for her, using abilities that came from years of hard study and one that gave such hope to other people that maybe their loved ones could be brought back to them.

7

9th May 1978 Polizia di Stato, Milan

It was early afternoon at the imposing headquarters of the Milan State Police and the majority of its impressive work force were gathered around an array of televisions and portable radios. Something had grabbed the attention of the whole Police Force.

Agente Vincenzo Rappelli and his colleagues were huddled around their chief's television taking in the news that Christian Democrat President Aldo Moro's body had just been recovered in the boot of an abandoned car in Via Caetani, Rome. The car had been left midway between the Christian Democratic Party and the Communist Party Headquarters, in defiance of the police, who had been keeping all of Italy under strict surveillance since the President's kidnapping fifty-four days earlier. The organisation responsible, Brigate Rosse was a paramilitary organization seeking to create a revolutionary state by terrorist means - sabotage and violent attacks on government officials and civilians to create an atmosphere of unease and destabilisation in Italy. Frequent attacks of violence, especially kneecapping victims whilst going about their normal daily travels, bank robberies and kidnapping were keeping the cities of Italy in a state of constant fear. Milan was a particular target, as it was seen as a hive of corrupt government officials and of both commerce and imperialist ideals.

Brigate Rosse was made of up of young radicals who supported communism in its most extreme form. Excluded from the legitimate political parties they needed to finance their movement by robberies and drug-trafficking but strongly claimed to have support nonetheless from legitimate left wing parties and later this was argued as one of the reasons they were so successful.

With all this political activity, the Milanese Police force were under intense pressure to calm an increasingly nervous city. Today's news was a major headache for them and the expected reaction would have to be controlled immediately.

The officers waited patiently to receive their orders from Ispettore Capo Bruno. The small stature of the middle-aged, bald man belied the enormous influence the inspector had over the station and his men. Partly because of his connections but mainly due to his outstanding ability to solve crimes at an extraordinary rate, he had earned loyalty and respect from his men.

Reports were already coming in of large crowds gathering at the metro stations and moving towards Piazza del Duomo. The shops surrounding it and in the arcadia, were pulling their shutters down and their owners were getting away as fast as they could. Business was over for the day. Brigate Rosse were about to achieve their goal for the day, mass disruption and the full attention of the police over the whole country.

Bruno announced that every available agente was to take up positions at each central station and around the city centre to try to disperse as many of the excitable crowds as possible. They would have to allow the citizens to demonstrate their grief for the loss of their popular leader and of course the Cathedral would be packed to capacity as prayers were said for his soul and carried by loudspeakers to the shocked crowd outside in the square. However, they would also have to deal with the supporters of this Brigate Rosse triumph over a so-called fascist regime - were young students in the main. The armed police presence would hopefully discourage any violence they might want to cause in support.

Vincenzo Rappelli and his partner Arno Tassi strapped on their shoulder holstered guns and made their way to their police car along with the others in their team. There was an air of excited, adrenalin-fuelled anticipation as they sped off.

The tension in the air around the square was electric. People were openly weeping and praying whilst others were shouting victory for the people. It was a fierce struggle for the police to maintain control, but with the arrest of several aggressors and the obvious threat of armed police ready to shoot, the majority of the defiant youths eventually admitted defeat and slunk off into the background whilst the prayers and sorrowful cries continued into early evening.

A few officers were injured by stones hurled as missiles but on the whole the operation had been a success and they all headed back to headquarters except for those with an ongoing duty to keep an eye out for further trouble.

Vincenzo and Arno got back to their desks just before clocking off time. They had completed a twelve-hour shift and, whilst consuming the sandwiches and hot coffee provided for the returning officers, they were sitting around discussing the day or dealing with all the other matters that had come in during the day. Vincenzo and the others also needed to quickly but carefully write up their statements to protect themselves from the many claims of police brutality bound to ensue from those who'd been arrested in the days that followed.

It was just after nine. Arno had already left, and Vincenzo was about to follow when he heard a commotion coming from downstairs at Reception. He quickly picked up his gun and slid it back into his holster before sprinting to the stairs. As the State Police Headquarters of Milan, possible terrorist strikes were always in the front of every police officer's mind and all were trained to be prepared for such an eventuality at any minute.

Vincenzo stood listening, hidden behind a wall at the top of the stairs. From the raised voices floating upwards he realised it was cries of distress not violence he could hear. Making his way downstairs he was shocked to see a well-known face — that of the minister for the Regione Lombardia, Marcello Buscolli. Accompanied by his wife he was demanding to see Ispettore Capo Bruno immediately.

"Vite! Vite! I demand attention now! My son is missing. He was out all day with the nanny and they have not returned. They may have got caught up in the demonstration. The stupid girl is ignorant of our politics. They may be hurt or lost. Get your officers to look for them immediately! Why the hell didn't she stay near home instead of going shopping as usual. She will be sent home on the first flight when she returns!"

"Try to stay calm Signor Buscolli and I will fetch the Capo. Ah…Officer Rappelli. He will escort you upstairs and we can sort it out. I'm sure you will find that they are simply delayed in returning home. English girls are more fool-hardy than our girls as you know. She would not have understood what was happening in the square and has most likely taken refuge in some café while she waits to come home. Do not worry, both of you."

Vincenzo led them up to Bruno's office, and explained to his boss what had happened. Then he quietly shut the door and left for the evening, shaking his head and sighing to himself. What a day this had been and what now?

He sincerely hoped that the Buscolli child and his English nanny would already be back home.

8
2008 – Polizia di Stato, Milan.

"I was to be disappointed as you know. What happened in the following days is well-documented in the case files and as young officers with less than five years' service, Arno and I were partnered with more experienced members of the crime unit. We were only involved on the periphery of operations of course, mainly dealing with incoming information and sifting out the false leads, of which there were many, and dispatching the hopeful ones to our older partners. We were not involved with any decision making or strategy.

"On the second day Kate Marshall and Luca were officially declared missing. The Buscollis made a plea on the local news channel, alongside Ispettore Capo Bruno, for any information regarding any sighting on the ninth of May, of the missing nanny and child and to beg for their release if they were being held against their will. Meanwhile, because of the high profile of the child's father, as many of the police force as possible, were out searching for them.

"On the third day a journalist on the local Milanese daily paper, Signor Gianni Bianchi, received a letter stating that Luca Buscolli and his nanny had been taken for ransom by members of the Brigate Rosse because of the actions of his corrupt father and that they would be in touch with Marcello Buscolli to discuss a deal.

"All hell broke loose at the station when Signor Bianchi brought the letter discreetly to us on the understanding that he would be allowed to cover the story exclusively for the paper. After a complete dressing down from Bruno concerning his loose morals and disregard for the safety of the child, a deal was struck that no information about this turn of events would be leaked to the public. The operation to take the ransom note seriously and set into motion a recovery and payment plan was taken over by the Special Operations force who dealt with political crimes. From something in the ransom note they had confirmed it to be genuine.

"The kidnappers stated their demands in several phone calls, finally allowing the police to speak to Kate to make sure she was still alive and for Signor Buscolli to confirm that the voice was hers. She assured them that she and Luca were well but scared and begged him to pay the ransom as quickly as possible. Then she was cut off and negotiations commenced between Special Op's Forces and the kidnappers.

"As you know the handover went tragically wrong and the kidnappers were shot and killed in the process along with two dedicated officers so, of course, the police were left with no one to tell us where they had hidden Kate and Luca.

"It was a total disaster and a deep embarrassment for Special Op's Forces, who could not understand how it had gone so wrong.

"Again, we received many hoax calls claiming to know where the captives were being held thanks to the media reporting on the whole fiasco and Signor Bianchi lost his exclusivity straight away, much to his despair.

"We were much hindered by the workload of false information as you might expect but finally after several weeks an anonymous phone call, claiming to be from a gang member, again containing a piece of identifying information that the Special Forces considered legitimate, was received at the station. It declared that Kate Marshall and Luca Buscolli were dead. What is more, it implicated Kate as being part of the kidnapping, a supposition that had been gathering momentum in the press and among the Milanese population. It was claimed that the killing had been done in retaliation for their fallen comrades.

"After that, despite all of us working tirelessly on any and every trivial lead that might arise, the case was eventually wound down and finally consigned to the unsolved files, now called cold cases and the two captives were assumed to be, indeed, dead.

"The files will show you all this in detail, but I thought it might be helpful for you to hear my interpretation of those sad days. You are most welcome to study the files with fresh eyes. Maybe you will see something that we did not. There is always that hope."

Jasmine and Maddie had sat rapt in his recollections of the crime and both felt he was still upset that the little boy had never been found.

Jasmine asked if he had also suspected Kate as being part of the kidnap plot and he answered that, truthfully, he did not know and perhaps would never do so and it still worried him even after all these years. They continued chatting over another cup of delicious expresso until finally, Vincenzo said, "I must bid you goodbye and get on with my working day but my wife insists I invite you to dinner this evening at my home."

They graciously accepted and left, their arms laden with enough dusty boxes of files to keep them busy for the foreseeable future.

Vincenzo had organized a taxi to pick Jasmine and Maddie up from their apartment at 7.30 p.m. They were ready, having spent the day organising the files into two separate piles to share the work load and then, begun the laborious task of reading through each piece of information in minute detail, always hoping for something to jump out at one of them that others had missed.

Later, they spent some time debating what to wear - formal, smart, casual? Vincenzo hadn't given any indication of which would be appropriate so they eventually settled for smart but summery shift dresses and matching shoes, Jasmine in navy and Maddie in a sumptuous cerise number that showed off the gloriously tanned skin she had acquired on a sunbed much to Jasmine's horror and her doom-laden prophesies involving skin cancer statistics. She would rather be pale and interesting she proclaimed then take the risk but did concede that her friend looked amazing.

Vincenzo's home was on the outskirts of Milan city centre, near the San Siro Stadium where football matches and horse racing were held. Parts of the area, they noticed had become rundown; old apartment buildings and factories left to rot over the years apparently. It would seem Milan had fallen victim to the declining economy as much as the rest of Europe. It was sad to see such neglect so close to the affluent city centre.

Fortunately, although modest in comparison with the apartment that the women were staying in, Vincenzo and his family lived in a large apartment building surrounded by high fencing and a security guard at the gate, who quickly allowed the taxi in on confirming that they were expected. Jasmine and Maddie got out and made their way to the second floor where they were greeted by Vincenzo's wife. She was a petite, attractive woman, probably in her late forties, and she welcomed them into her home graciously saying she was so pleased to have English guests for a change instead of Vincenzo's usual work colleagues who were always willing to sit at the Rappellis' dinner table whether invited by her or not, she said, accompanied by a good-natured chuckle. She introduced herself as Julietta and said that her three youngest boys would not be joining them as they had already eaten and were busy doing their homework but her eldest Vincenzo junior, whom they called Enzo, was eager to meet them. Jasmine and

Maddie followed her into a large modern living space that incorporated the kitchen area, dining area and seating arranged around a large television. Julietta ushered them towards a large dining table that was already prepared with a variety of dishes containing little appetizers that were usually part of the Italian cuisine, Julietta informed the two women. She filled their glasses with a light, refreshing white wine and bid them make themselves at home whilst she got on with the meal. Vincenzo and his son joined them, abandoning a football match that had been on the television and greeted them enthusiastically. Enzo was a younger version of his father, handsome and looked to be about thirty years old. He chatted away, putting Jasmine and Maddie at ease and soon the atmosphere around the table was lively and entertaining. Vincenzo informed them, proudly, that his son was also a policeman and was currently directing traffic as part of his training but hoped to follow in his father's footsteps and become an inspector. He had come late to the police force, having gone into the army first. However, he had decided a military career was not for him, after all.

"Believe me, a traffic controller in Milan is not without its dangers" Enzo said, with a hearty laugh. "I am looking forward to the day when I can join my father in a less stressful part of policing," he joked.

Throughout the lengthy meal they all spoke of the case, with Julietta contributing her memories of the time but unable to be of any further help, only to offer her opinion that Kate and Luca had died shortly after their abduction as most Milanese had thought, at the time. She was interested in hearing Jasmine and Maddie's plans to search for witnesses from 1978, and they confessed that they would be up all night making a list of possible leads from Vincenzo's case files and start their search for clues tomorrow. Enzo professed his eagerness to help them on his time off from traffic control as he would relish the chance to get his teeth into some detective work and the two women agreed that his help would be welcome along with his father's, especially as Milan was unfamiliar to them.

As the meal drew to a close, they talked of lighter things and Jasmine and Maddie got to know more about the Rappelli family. Julietta explained that there was fifteen years between the birth of Enzo and their other three boys, Marco who was fifteen and her thirteen years old twins Roberto and Nunzio. She praised God for the miracle of her boys as she had no idea why they had not been blessed again for such a long time after Enzo but admitted that she was not entirely enamoured with having three teenagers to deal with at her time of life, she chuckled, good naturedly. After a leisurely coffee and exquisite limoncello liquor, Vincenzo ordered a taxi and his family bid them goodnight. The three teenagers had made a brief appearance to say hello to the English guests and Jasmine and Maddie had been impressed by their good manners. The boys were all a mixture of the genes of their mother and father whereas Enzo was so like his father. Jasmine had to admit to herself that she was taken by him already and was looking forward to having his company whilst in Milan. When they returned to their apartment, Maddie brewed up strong coffee and they set about making the list of people that they were anxious to make contact with. It was a long night for them both but at last they retired to bed exhausted but excited about tomorrow when their search would really begin.

9

9th May 1978. Piazza del Duomo, Milan

KATE was quickly led away from the Piazza by Raphael who was carrying a smiling Luca in his arms. The child was familiar with the man holding him and seemed to feel more relaxed with him than with a panicked Kate who was distressed by the confusion around her. She had no idea where they were going either and wasn't sure if she should stick with her boyfriend or just try to make her way back home as quickly as possible. Raphael hadn't given her any time to assess the situation really but she trusted him; after all he was much more aware than she was of what was taking place and how quickly they should get away from the gathering crowd.

She followed him, holding on to his shirt, anxious not to let Luca out of her sight or to become separated from the two of them and soon they were in the relative quiet of a suburban street where Raphael came to a stop and gestured to Kate to follow him into a little café where he was greeted by one of the friends Kate had met before. They sat down at a table and Luca was given a drink to occupy him as the two men, talking too rapidly for Kate to follow, fell into conversation.

She was beginning to feel anxious again as she had no idea where they were and she was, after all, in charge of Luca's welfare. She tried to get some understanding of the discussion that was going on. Raphael seemed to be getting annoyed with his friend who was repeatedly shaking his head in disagreement with him. It appeared, if she was translating correctly, that Raphael wanted to take Kate and Luca somewhere with his friend but the friend was reluctant to agree? Kate wasn't happy with the turn of events either.

"Raphael", she interrupted. "What's going on please? I think I should wait here for a while and then head to Il Duomo and make my way back towards the metro and head home for today. I am sure that is what my employers will be expecting me to do if they're aware of the demonstration."

The two men stopped talking and looked at her. Raphael came and sat down beside her and the friend went into the back of the café. *He evidently works here then*, thought Kate, absently.

"I do not think that is a good idea, Caro. Things could be getting ugly there. You do not understand the passion of the Italian people. We feel very angry about our politics, you must understand. It is better that you stay with me and I will take you back to your apartment. Gianni, my friend there, is calling our other friend who has a car to come and collect us. Do not worry, Caro. You are safe with me you know that. Are we not in love?" he said, kissing her gently on the mouth and giving Luca a pat on the cheek. The child gazed adoringly up at him and Kate smiled and relaxed a little; of course she safe with him. She hadn't known him for long, but she felt good in his company and trusted him and it would be easier to go home by car. It wouldn't take them long and she would probably be home before her employers realised she had been anywhere near the demonstration. It would be better if she did not have to admit that she had placed Luca in any kind of danger, anyway.

It was not long before the promised car drew up outside the café and Raphael bundled Kate and Luca into the back seats as he sat in the front with the driver who looked to be another student of the same age as Raphael. As he glanced back through the rear-view mirror at Kate, she recognised him as one of several friends that had accompanied her on her other days out with Raphael. She smiled at him but he did not respond, staring with fixed eyes on the road ahead.

Soon they were speeding along the dual carriageway leading away from the city and Kate's anxiety returned as she realised that the two men were not taking her back to the apartment. She started to protest but Raphael told her to calm herself as he knew best. He said something rapidly to the driver who once again scowled into the rear mirror.

Kate was in danger of panicking now. What the hell had she done getting in the car with Luca, a child she was solely responsible for. But surely Raphael knew what he was doing didn't he? she argued with herself, and she trusted him, didn't she?

As they continued Kate realised she was truly lost and totally reliant on her boyfriend. She tried to hold down her panic and asked him, in a calmer voice, "Where are we going Raphael? It's getting quite late and Luca must be hungry. My employer will be expecting us home for our meal. We always eat together as she likes to spend time with Luca and Santa, her daughter, at the table. I was hoping I wouldn't need to mention I'd been at Il Duomo as she'll be angry with me. What's happening? Why are we travelling in the opposite direction?"

"Shut up, you stupid little girl!" roared the driver. "Raph keep her quite or I will do it for you!"

Kate was stunned with shock, as the magnitude of what had just been said, hit her.

Raphael said something, quickly, to the driver then shouted "Basta! I will deal with this. Keep your eyes on the road."

He looked back at a scared-looking Kate and spoke sternly to her. "You will understand shortly. Please stay silent or I cannot say what he will do. He is not as kind hearted as I and you and the boy are nothing to him. When we arrive, there will be people who speak good English not like I and then you will learn why you have been taken on this special day that has become very lucky for us."

Taken!

The word screamed inside Kate's skull. *My God what the hell's happening?* Her mind simply could not connect with the idea that her boyfriend has suddenly turned into someone who had just threatened her and an infant. It wasn't possible but there was no other explanation. Her whole body began to react with this awful realization and she started to shake uncontrollably and then screamed at the top of her voice.

Luca stared at her and began howling in alarm.

The car stopped abruptly and the driver turned around in his seat to face her. "You! Stop now or I will slit your throat, understand!" He made a slicing gesture across his own throat. "We do not need you, we have the boy. You! Raph, get in the back and keep her quiet."

Kate stared at Raphael, her boyfriend, the person that had made her time in this big city far from home, exciting and new and who she had been falling in love with. It wasn't possible. Surely, he could never harm her and Luca? He must be in trouble with this other man in some way and she had merely been dragged into the situation by being with him today of all days. She tried to think logically, despite her state of fear. If she remained silent and did not distress Luca all would be made clear soon enough. Raphael would not harm them, she convinced herself, again.

All became quiet as they proceeded along the country roads to their destination. They drove on for what seemed an eternity to Kate before the car started to slow down and they turned into a long narrow lane that lead up to what seemed to be a derelict farm and outbuildings.

The car stopped and the two men got out. Raphael gathered Luca, who had fallen asleep, into his arms whilst the driver grabbed Kate and manhandled her roughly towards a side door in the furthest outbuilding, telling her not to open her mouth or he would shut it for her. What Kate encountered next was beyond her comprehension, she turned to look at Raphael and he had the grace to hang his head and turn away from her. She was in hell, she realised. The cold stark building seemed to be crowded with people, possibly her age or a little older, all dressed in army-like combat gear, five men and two women. They all turned to look at the new arrivals coming through the door. One of the men strode up to Raphael and gave him a pat on the back and then hugged him in a gesture that was obviously congratulatory. The others all began to talk amongst themselves with great excitement and too fast for Kate to understand what was being said.

Kate felt totally numb, too traumatised to take in her situation and sank to the floor too weak to stand. One of the women came swiftly over and helped her up, whilst the other took Luca, who was still asleep and laid him onto a heap of blankets in the corner of the room.

"You will be alright as long as you do as we say and keep the boy quiet. We do not wish to harm you but we will if you do not co-operate. You have been kidnapped for ransom from your corrupt bastido of an employer. You do not realise who you work for, I think. He is a man not worthy of the comfortable life his family leads so we have decided his dishonest money can help our cause to fight the Fascists of this State. He pays, we give back his son, simple," said the dark-haired woman who had picked Kate up from the floor. She led Kate over to Luca and shoved her roughly down beside the sleeping boy. Kate looked on, full of guilt at what she had led this little boy into through sheer ignorance and stupidity. She had behaved as she would at home and never once considered that she was in a foreign country with different customs and ideals. She would have to pay the price now, please God not at the cost of their lives.

Even she knew that ransom demands were fraught with danger and just because, of course, her employer would pay for his son, what about her? Then, slowly, the thought hit like a blow, she had seen them all. None of them had bothered to hide their faces. She was

Raphael's girlfriend, wasn't she? She wasn't meant to come out of this alive to lead the police to them. They would almost certainly kill her.

As she sat cradling Luca, the tears fell silently onto her cheeks as she watched Raphael act as if he didn't know her, as he celebrated the group's success with gusto.

10

May 10ᵗʰ, 1978

KATE was surprised to find that she had actually fallen asleep sometime in the night and had been awoken by the sound of activity in the large room. She glanced beside her to see Lucas was not there. She scanned the room and saw the woman that had carried him to the blankets, the night before, sitting at a table feeding him. He looked quite happy, *so at least*, thought Kate, *he's in no immediate danger*. She sat up, stiff, having spent the night on the floor, and called out to the woman for a drink of water.

"Come" replied the woman, beckoning her towards the table. The men were nowhere about but the other woman was making coffee on a small utility table. She turned around and handed Kate a cup. "Here, drink," she ordered, curtly.

Kate sat down at the table next to Luca, who raised his arms to be taken onto her lap, which she did. He smiled up at her and said her name, and asked when they would go home in his infant's rudimentary language. He always spoke English to Kate but Italian to anyone else, already able to differentiate between the two tongues.

She cuddled him and kissed his little head and told him, "Soon Caro, soon." This seemed to satisfy him and he continued eating a biscuit he'd been given.

"What is going to happen to us?" Kate asked the two women. "Where is Raphael? Why has he done this to us?"

"Nothing will happen today. The men are out on their daily business. We do not wish to attract attention, of course. We will go shortly too and you will stay here. We will return this evening. Tomorrow, the ransom will be demanded. Do not concern yourself with Raph. He cares nothing for you, foolish English girl. He cares who you look after, a politician's children," the dark- haired woman said, with a cruel smirk on her face.

The lighter haired, shorter bulkier woman had in the meanwhile made her a sandwich and now gave it to her with some of the biscuits Luca had been eating. "Here, eat," she said abruptly.

Kate wasn't sure if this was her manner or if she couldn't speak English as well as the other woman.

11

KATE awoke to the sound of loud animated voices and marvelled at her ability to sleep so soundly through her ordeal. *Am I being given sleeping pills in the drinks?* she wondered.

Everyone was seated around the table whilst Franco seemed to be giving out instructions to everyone. As Kate sat up she could see Luca playing beside them with his new toys, oblivious to any danger. She quickly used the bathroom and picked Luca up to greet him the way she always did at home with a cuddle and a kiss on his head. "Ciao Luca."

"Ciao Kate, look my toys," the little boy replied with a huge grin on his face. *He will be okay*, Kate prayed silently. *They will not harm him, surely; the ransom will be paid and he'll go home to his family.*

Franco called her to the table. "Come here, sit," he demanded. "There has been a plea on the television by the Buscollis and polizia for contact. The whole world knows of your capture and are talking about our cause. We have sent a demand to a journalist on Milano's leading paper so now it begins. If all goes as planned, you will be exchanged for the money and that is that. Continue to cooperate and you will survive this."

How? thought Kate, in panic. *I know you now. I am a danger to you all.* Would they leave her somewhere remote so that by the time she was discovered they would be long gone? That was her only hope. She realised she must concentrate and try to understand what they said to each other if she was to have any hope of surviving this nightmare. So far, they had not harmed her in any way so she must appeal to their humanity when the time came for the changeover. She would not be handed over she was certain, but at least little Luca would be safe.

Throughout the day the members of the gang came and went and she realised it was Saturday and they were not required to be at University, or wherever they went in their normal, everyday lives. Stefana, Carla and Raphael spoke frequently to her and made sure Luca and herself had eaten and drank enough throughout the day. Kate tried to find out any information that might help her but, although the three were in a state of excitement, they just told her not to worry but to do as Franco said and she would be ok.

Finally, towards sunset, Franco and the driver, Beppe, arrived back from wherever they had been all day. Franco beckoned Carla over to them and a rapid conversation ensued. Then Carla called Raphael over and again there was earnest conversation between them all.

Raphael made his way over to Kate, who was feeding Luca an evening meal in preparation for settling the tired little boy to sleep for the night.

"Kate, we have made contact with your employers. They wish to have proof that you are alive. That is understandable, yes? You will go with us to make a telephone call when the child is asleep. He will be safe with Stefana. You will tell them that you and the boy are safe and well. Then the exchange will happen tomorrow. Luca will be returned and I have asked that you will be released when we are safely away from here. That is the best I can do for you. I must warn you that people are questioning your part in the kidnapping. Do not make things difficult for yourself." Raphael explained all this in a mixture of English and Italian, as it was the way in which they had always communicated with each other.

How could I have thought myself in love with this man? she berated herself.

When Luca was asleep and settled for the night in his blankets Stefana lay down beside him and read a book. She'd come prepared for boredom it seemed to Kate. She had offered her a book earlier in the evening but Kate's Italian wasn't up to it or indeed, her frame of mind.

Franco, Beppe and Raphael accompanied Kate in the car, Raphael sitting in the back with her. As they drove off Raphael said sorry and then put a sack of some sort over her head and pushed her down onto the floor. They could not risk anyone seeing her with them.

They drove on for some miles until the car pulled up beside a public phone box. They waited a few minutes to check that the area was deserted and then Franco got out and Raphael removed the sack and pulled Kate upright and out of the car. Franco took hold of her arm and took her rapidly to the phone box closing the door behind them. He then put his arms around her shoulder, as if they were girlfriend and boyfriend, just in case anyone should come by.

"Now, Kate. You will speak to Marcello Buscolli for only a few seconds. You will say that that you and Luca are safe and unharmed. That we have treated you well and you will be returned if the ransom is paid. That is all. Any attempt to identify us will result in your death and Luca will not be found. Do you understand?"

She nodded that she did.

He proceeded to dial a number that he had on a scrap of paper. It was picked up immediately. The Buscollis, and probably the police, would have been waiting the last two days for this moment, obviously, thought Kate as she stood cramped inside the phone box beside her captor.

Franco spoke rapidly and then shoved the telephone into her hands, with a warning glare. "Speak!" he commanded.

"This is Kate Marshall, your nanny. Luca and I are well and being looked after you must not worry too much but please pay the ransom I beg you. You will recognise my voice and, as proof that it is me, Luca has a birthmark on his thigh shaped like a diamond and I am so sorry Signor."

The phone was snatched away from her and put back in place. Franco shoved her out of the phone box and hit her across the face. "I said no information! Disobey me again and you are gone, understand?"

"Yes, I understand," she replied, rubbing her cheek and trying not to cry.

They got back in the car and Raphael placed the sack over her head again and returned her to the floor of the car.

Beppe asked if all had gone well and Franco nodded in silence.

When they returned to the outbuildings Raphael helped her out and spoke to the waiting gang, outlining what had happened and explaining Kate's swollen cheek. Stefana came over to her and ushered her into the bathroom to put cold water on her face. When they came out Raphael, Franco and Renzo had gone off again in the car. Probably to make the arrangements for the ransom pickup tomorrow, Kate surmised. Soon this will be over one way or the other, she thought resignedly, as she sat at the table and drank the milky coffee Stefana had made her, more than likely laced with sleeping pills, for which Kate was actually grateful. She didn't want to lie awake thinking of the next day as it might be her last.

She did not hear the men return a few hours later or the furtive conversations between the gang members as they went about deciding her and Luca's futures. She was sleeping the sleep of the innocent.

combination. He hoped for the former who would at least be professional and operating with the sole aim of getting the ransom and escaping without a murder charge hanging over their heads.

The convoy quickly moved out of the affluent city centre and to the more industrial areas and outlying farmland. Fortunately, the phone box wasn't too far away and set in a rural area with a limited population, who still needed a public telephone.

Giordano instructed the drivers of the three cars, via their walkie-talkies to cease following Marcello's car and to position themselves as a road block in each direction away from the area and await further instructions. Officers positioned in the undergrowth surrounding the phone box were to be vigilant and on standby.

Time went slowly and Marcello's nerves were at breaking point, as he feverishly stared at the innocuous phone box, willing it to ring. His car windows were open in the intense heat and he would be able to rush to pick up the phone as soon as it did ring. Nonetheless, he jumped with fright when it did. He hastily rushed inside the phone box and grabbed the receiver, shouting, "I'm here, ready."

A male voice replied, "That is good," and gave specific instructions to continue driving until he came to a bridge above a small dried up river bed and, again, warned that if he did not come alone Luca would be killed along with the nanny.

Marcello said, "Of course, Please do not harm my son. I am completely alone."

"You are not alone. They are following you even if you do not know. Look around Minister and get rid of them or the deal is off. You have one hour to get to the bridge. That is all. Good luck Minister." The voice abruptly ended the call.

"Bastardi!" screamed Marcello, nearly pulling the receiver from the wall. He stood outside the phone box and scanned the surrounding area. At first it looked deserted but he still shouted "Bastardi! Where are you? Make yourselves known. They know you have followed me! My son is at stake! I will go on alone do you understand? Or you will all face the consequences!"

A full minute passed before someone stood up from the scrub grass further along from the roadside. Then another and another. Giordano had given them instructions to show themselves, conceding that the game was up.

The nearest agente approached Marcello and handed him his walkie-talkie.

"Sir, I realise you are very angry and scared but you need us. We cannot allow them to escape. You must know this. They have not seen us and are just assuming that we would be involved. We are very good at our job. Please trust me," Giordano pleaded.

"I cannot take the risk, Giordano. You know that too. Stay away! My bodyguard is all I need. If my son is put in any more danger I will personally see that you never work again. Is that clear?" With that, he ripped off the wire taped to his body and threw it to the ground.

"Yes, Minister," replied Giordano, non-committally, having heard this many, many times from others. He had his orders from a higher source than this man.

"I will continue alone, do not attempt to follow," Marcello demanded.

"As you wish, but you are not doing your son any great service. I hope you do not live to regret your actions, Minister Buscolli."

"I will be the judge of that, not you," Marcello barked, handing the walkie-talkie back to the police and returning to his car. He left a trail of dust in his wake as he sped off.

Time for Plan B, thought Giordano.

This was it. All Giordano's officers were on high alert, adrenalin pumping through their veins.

The car stopped some distance away from Marcello's and blocking the view of the bridge. A car door opened and one masked man dropped down to the riverbed to retrieve the case and swiftly returned to the car, unseen by the hidden officers but not by Marcello.

Everyone had been expecting the nanny and child to be handed over as soon as the money had been checked, but nothing happened and it seemed that the kidnappers were preparing to take off immediately, or at least that is what it seemed like to a distraught Marcello. The officers too were awaiting instructions. They had expected the back doors of the car to open and release the child and nanny and for the kidnappers to speed off and make their escape.

Meanwhile Franco had calmly checked the contents of the case and was about to instruct Beppe to start up the car and blast continuously on the horn, the signal for Carla to approach and release the child where he could be seen by his father and still give them time to escape, whilst he ran to him. This was the most dangerous time but he had not been able to think of an easier way to complete the handover and, of course, for a minute or so, the minister would panic and think they were reneging on the deal, but in case the police were there, this was the only means of escape. It would be less than a minute before Carla came into sight and Marcello would see his son and forget about them, that was the plan anyway.

However, he had not counted on Marcello's volatile temper and all hell breaking loose.

Marcello was not accustomed to being thwarted and had expected his son to be there in the car. Realising that he was not, he stormed out of his own vehicle and charged over to the kidnappers' car to confront them.

He was immediately followed by an alert bodyguard trying to take control of the situation, gun drawn to protect his employer.

Marcello grabbed the passenger's door handle and yanked it open.

Beppe tried desperately to start the car but could now see police officers approaching, seemingly from nowhere.

"Bastardos! Bastardos! Where is Luca! I will kill you!" Marcello screamed, now holding a gun that he had carefully hidden and pointing it at Franco's head.

Franco told the driver to get out of there and tried to push the gun away banking on Marcello's inexperience with firearms and, aiming his own gun at Marcello, pulled the trigger.

The shot hit Marcello in the arm and he cried out, dropping his own gun. In that split second the bodyguard dived in front of his boss and began to fire indiscriminately into the car.

Franco was hit directly in the head and Beppe in the chest. Renzotook multiple shots and Raphael was bleeding copiously from an obviously fatal wound to the throat.

Within seconds all four men were dead with Giordano and his officers powerless to stop the carnage.

The bodyguard dropped his gun to attend to his boss who was lying on the ground screaming his son's name, in vain. Luca had not been in the car and neither had Kate.

Giordano ordered the bodyguard to drop to the ground and quickly handcuffed him, then released him to the awaiting officers who read him his rights.

This was a catastrophe. Giordano gazed down at the broken father and listened in despair to his sobs for a moment before asking one of his men to call the shooting in and the female agente to help Marcello into her car and return to headquarters.

Then he silently stood waiting for the chaos that would descend upon him. He would be called to account for this disaster, as he was well aware, not least of all by Marcello Buscolli. His own conscience led him to pray desperately that he would not have to add Luca and Kate to the list of lives he had inadvertently extinguished by allowing the minister's power to overrule his own common sense and to refuse to let a father do his own negotiations in a ransom deal.

They had both been foolish beyond belief and must now pay the price. He glanced inside the car at the dead men. *Boys really*, he thought with real sadness.

her new life experience. The job would be for six months initially but would continue indefinitely if both parties were agreeable.

The agency was paid and all was settled.

Kate got on a flight to Milan with more than a little trepidation, but plenty of excitement to compensate, and no knowledge of where she would be living for the next six months. Originally, she had wanted to go to a coastal resort in any country but the Buscolli family had a coastal villa as well as their Milanese home, that they retired to when the summer heat of the city got too much for its occupants so she would be getting the best of both worlds and Signora Buscolli informed her there would be skiing in winter too. Kate couldn't believe her luck and since it was to be an adventure, the location didn't really matter too much to Kate who was known for her spontaneity or, some might say, foolhardiness.

The first days in Milan had been a major culture shock for her.

Most obviously, no one seemed to speak English except for her employers and she was encouraged to attempt to ask for things in shops in Italian, as Italians found this endearing when you tried and would take their time to help a struggling foreigner, Francesca had smilingly informed her.

Milan was a vibrant upmarket massive city, the epitome of high fashion and culture and Kate couldn't help feeling dowdy and gauche as the models paraded by on their fashion shoots almost daily, but it was a new and exciting world nonetheless and she couldn't wait to explore all the clothes shops with her first week's pay. The buildings were magnificent and Kate, coming from a suburban midlands town, was awestruck at the beauty surrounding her, as she took Luca to the old palace parks and museums to occupy her day. Although Luca was too young to appreciate his surroundings as yet, she was taking the opportunity to get to know her new home. She quickly realised, however, that her Italian counterparts were not given the freedom to move around alone as she was used to doing. Italian men were often a little too forward in their compliments and wandering hands on the tube. Italian girls and woman did not go out alone in the evening either and Kate was lucky to have been introduced to other English nannies by her employer, Francesca's friends and acquaintances, or she would have been very lonely in those first few months.

She discovered there was a very large nanny network who met up all the time in an English style pub in the centre of town and that was where she went on her nights off. She had become very good friends with a couple of them. Amy was twenty and from Lancashire and Lynne was, like her, only eighteen and she came from a small village in Scotland. They met up most days with their charges and it made it fun to be all together with the children playing whilst they chatted.

Kate settled quickly into her new life and was happy. Francesca spoke in English to her and the maid Marietta could speak English having learnt it at school but mostly Kate got by, gradually understanding more and more Italian and using hand gestures copiously to make herself understood. The months slipped by and soon she was as much a part of the family and its life as if she had always been there. She adored Luca who was busy babbling away in a mixture of Italian and English and was fond of Santa although finding her a little spoilt and secretly suspecting that the child regarded her as a mere servant. She had heard Francesca chastise her one evening for something she had said to her father about the staff including Kate. Kate was a little hurt but really, she supposed Santa was right; she was staff and was treated differently because she lived in and Marietta and the cook, Signora Tutti, did not.

Inevitably, most of the nannies came to have Italian boyfriends. The complete absence of parental control had something to do it, and of course, they all came flocking to the enlightened English girls even if they would in the main eventually choose a *good* Italian girl to marry.

Kate had met Raphael when she was with her friends sitting on the steps of Il Duomo where foreign tourists and Italian students congregated in the hot sun along with what seemed like thousands of pigeons. Everyone met up on their nights off and let their boyfriends show them the Milanese nightlife. It was all so exciting to young girls totally alone in a big city.

Kate saw little of Marcello Buscolli as he spent most of his days in Parliament and never returned until long after Kate and the rest of the family had all retired. Francesca also spent much of the day out. Kate didn't know where she went unless they visited friends at the weekend together or very occasionally Marcello accompanied them for an outdoor meal in the grounds of an old farmhouse, under the shade of cooling trees, all so bohemian to Kate and surreal.

In the evenings when Luca was in bed asleep, Kate would spend an hour with Santa helping with her English studies and Santa would attempt to coach Kate in some basic Italian but, frequently, Kate came to realise, gave her the wrong words on purpose. Santa wasn't really interested in Kate's company, preferring to be with her mama and papa if they were at home and she had a perfunctory relationship with her brother so Kate and Luca were usually left to their own devices.

On Kate's days off, Marietta, the maid, took over Luca's care, never Francesca. Soon the two became good friends and enjoyed gossiping about their employers and talking about their boyfriends, although Marietta was only allowed to see her Gianni in the presence of her family. They were going to marry soon and Kate had been invited to the wedding. Marietta was twenty-two years old and lived locally in the more working-class area on the outskirts of the city, in a tall rundown apartment block with her parents and younger siblings. The home was warm and welcoming and Kate enjoyed visiting the family often. It was helping her with Italian speech, although Francesca had pointed out that she was learning the local dialect and to speak only in English to Luca as he would learn his Italian from his own family.

The cook, Signora Tutti, was a woman in her fifties who spoke no English so there was little or no conversation to be had between her and Kate apart from basic commands involving the household duties. Marietta acted as a go-between when necessary, which wasn't often, as the signora didn't seem to approve of either of them and kept to herself.

So, the days and months continued in their pleasant pattern as the weather got hotter and the city grew more stifling and unbearable and people began to look forward to the annual industrial shutdown across the city in August, when those who could, escaped to the coast.

The Buscollis were going to their villa on the Riviera and Kate would be going too. Marietta told her how lucky she was and how beautiful the Riviera was and how she wished she was going but the Buscollis employed local girls to keep house so didn't need her, sadly.

The family would be spending two months by the sea. Kate couldn't wait. It would be Luca's first birthday whilst they were there and she wondered what sort of celebrations a minister's son would receive.

As they were all packing up for the journey she realised that once again Marcello would not be coming with them but would visit when he could.

It was then, whilst dining at Marietta's home for the last time until they returned to Milan, that Kate came to learn the Buscolli family's *Big Secret* - one that would alter Kate's life forever, had she but known it then, as she sat with her friend Marietta, gossiping as they always did after a good meal and a few glasses of wine.

Signora Tutti listened carefully but it seemed at first as though she would not reply. She was just sitting quietly continuing to knit and Jasmine realised she was retreating into the past, a past that must have been painful for her too, as she had loved the Marcello family and had remained with them, until Marcello Buscolli had been murdered and Francesca and Santa had moved to London.

Finally, she spoke. "A terrible time for us all, yes…not a time I wish to recall but as you are trying to give some comfort, although I cannot see how you will do so, for poor Santa I will try my best. I cannot say that I knew Kate well as we did not communicate except to greet each other or to give instructions from Signora Buscolli but she seemed a pleasant girl, if a little foolish and headstrong, as all these foreign girls seemed to be. No Italian family would have allowed their daughters to roam about the city at any time without a chaperone. She would come in at all hours, so La Signora told me and this would worry the family but they felt that they could only warn her to be careful, as they were her employers not her family. However, I did on one occasion, as I told the police in my statement thirty years ago, report Kate to La Signora as I had seen her in the daytime, whilst she was looking after Luca, accompanied by a young Italian boy. This was quickly dealt with, or so La Signora thought, by her forbidding Kate to meet with this person, whom she discovered was her boyfriend, whilst she was in charge of Luca. Of course, we all later learned that he was the one that helped kidnap and murder them.

"My God, how I grieved about that you must know. I asked myself for many years if I could have done more but we could not know that this girl would bring about such sorrow. Alas I have no more to tell you than is in my statement. Marietta was the one who was good friends with Kate so you should speak to her. She always professed that she was sure that Kate was entirely innocent and as much a victim as Luca. This angered the family so they sacked her not long after she gave her statement to the police. I kept in touch over the first few years but then we went our separate ways. I think we did not want to talk of the tragedy anymore and we had nothing else in common. I'm sorry I cannot be of help but if you do discover anything please contact me and let me know. I would not like to go to my grave not knowing what happened to the poor child - such a tragedy." She sighed, shaking her head, lost in her thoughts once again.

The three visitors thanked her for her memories and her time and said goodbye, agreeing to let her know the outcome of their search, as soon as it was completed.

Sadly, their visit had been fruitless but hopefully their call on Signora Marietta Dolci would be more revealing.

After a quick lunch break they headed out hoping to find her at home.

20

FORTUNATELY, Marietta was at home and welcomed them inside her attractive apartment. She said that she would be very happy to try and recall anything that might help solve the mystery, of the disappearance of Kate and Luca after all this time. Jasmine noticed, with interest, that Marietta did not say *murder* as Signora Tutti had done. Perhaps they would get to know more about the teenage Kate from this witness's memories.

Marietta spoke fluent English so, this time, Jasmine took charge and quickly explained why they had been asked to re-examine the case evoking from Marietta sympathy for Santa now having been left all alone in the world. Family was the most important thing in life, she professed, especially to Italians and she was sorry the Buscollis had been ripped apart in such a hideous way. She then asked, "How might I be of help?"

"It would be helpful to us if you could give us an idea of what Kate was like and how she got on with the family. Was she happy?" asked Jasmine.

"Oh yes, very happy. Of course a little homesick sometimes. That was only natural but she was treated as one of the family at all times and felt very comfortable with everyone. All she was required to do was look after Luca's needs and help Santa with her English study. No one could have loved that child more. She would never have knowingly put him in harm's way. You understand, she was a victim too. I would stake my life on that, although I seemed to be the only one at the time," she added bitterly. "I knew Kate better than all the family and she was a lovely, caring girl who obviously got mixed up in something she didn't understand. What interest would she have had with our government politics, I ask you? She was simply in love with a young man and acted freely, as she would have done in England. Poor, poor, Kate and God keep them both," she sniffed, clearly upset now.

"I'm sorry Signora I do not mean to upset you but anything you can recall now that you might not have remembered at the time or that you would not have wanted to say for any reason - fear of getting involved perhaps more than you had to. You were a young girl too, and understandably a little afraid."

"Yes…yes very afraid. You cannot imagine what it was like. We all felt like suspects but we were grieving for them both too, when we realised that they were probably dead. I was sacked for supporting my friend, so I stayed quiet and I could no longer work for families with this hanging over me so I had to find shop work to keep myself."

"Forgive me but why were you so insistent that Kate was innocent? You also do not seem convinced that they were murdered. Is there anything you can tell us now the case is long forgotten by most and the Buscollis are deceased that might make us think that too? It will go no further I promise and this agente is here in an unofficial capacity, I can assure you."

Marietta sighed heavily and stared into the distance for several minutes. The three visitors held their breath, sensing an important decision being made, whether to trust them or just let the past go. Finally, Marietta looked at each one separately and silently prayed that she was not unleashing chaos into her own life and let go of the secret that had haunted her for thirty years.

"I told Kate that Luca was not the Buscollis biological child."

Jasmine, Maddie and Enzo stared opened mouth at Marietta. Whatever they had expected, it was not that. Shocked silence filled the room and Marietta started to cry. Maddie went quickly to her and put her arms around the distressed woman, trying to soothe her with words of comfort, saying it was better to let go of secrets than live a life of fear of discovery and she truly believed that.

"Can you explain what you mean, Marietta? "Jasmine asked, when the tears had subsided and Maddie had made them all coffee to calm her down after this revelation, none of them sure how significant or even true it was.

"I hope I am not bringing even more distress to Santa by telling you this, so please I beg you, do not use this information if it is of no help to your investigation. Only I have always wondered if, perhaps, the real parents had taken back the child but of course the Buscollis made no reference to the fact that Luca was not their own child and so I purposely forgot that I knew too. My mother had found this out through her sister, who was living in the South and knew of the extended Buscolli family in Bari. I swore her to secrecy telling her that it would bring much trouble to us all, as Marcello Buscolli obviously did not want anyone to know. He was a powerful man, you understand, especially you, Agente Rappelli. Italy is not England and its laws and politics are not something to get involved in. I simply hid my secret and never thought that this day would come."

"We promise that your part in this investigation will remain with us, Marietta. Santa wants only to know what happened so that she can say goodbye to the past and get on with her life. She does not expect us to find Luca and Kate alive. That hope died long ago and I'm certain that if she knew, and indeed your information is true, of Luca's parentage she would have told me. I would not distress her by telling her this news unless it solved the mystery. Do you know who the real parents are supposed to be?"

"Yes, I do. Luca's mother was the daughter of Marcello Buscolli's sister and a young Bari man that worked for the family. The family - you understand what it meant also by that in the South of Italy. Bari was poor and run by the old Sicilian families and Signor Buscolli's sister was married to the local Mafioso boss. Their daughter was sixteen and the boy a little older and when it was discovered that she was pregnant, the family sent her away and the boy was never seen again. No one discussed it as this thing happened a lot and police turned a blind eye to crime in Bari. When the daughter returned she was soon married to one of her father's cousins and that was that. My mother heard the story many years later from a relative who worked for the Buscolli family in Bari at the time. Years later the whole Buscolli family emigrated to New York including the daughter and her husband and their children. When I began working for the Milanese Buscollis my mother asked me if they were related to the Bari Buscollis and then told me the story, when she realised that they were."

"I see, thank you," Jasmine replied. "What made you decide to share this information with Kate? Surely it was a very big secret to reveal to a relative stranger and it wasn't your secret to tell. It was risky to give a young girl such explosive details of her employers lives that you were not meant to be party to either. Knowing how powerful and influential Marcello Buscolli was, you could both have been in big trouble."

"I was too young and foolish and I know now that I should not have told her but we were good friends and spent many evenings together discussing the family. You know, moaning and laughing about incidents that had happened in the day. She was particularly upset the day Signora Tutti told Signora Buscolli about seeing her with Raphael. She had been severely scolded and warned that if she saw him again whilst with Luca she would be sacked. To console her and offer her sympathy, I remarked that she would never put Luca in danger as she loved him more than anyone in the whole family, and it was plain to see that Luca saw her more as his mama than Francesca, who could barely spend more than a few minutes with her son. Of course, it was all childish talk and we moaned about Francesca's seemingly lack of love for her child and enormous love of spending time in beauty salons and fine dining. We drank a bottle of wine and got a little merry; we were in a café close to the apartment and I suppose it loosened my tongue. Kate said how devastated she would be if she had to leave the Buscollis and she could not imagine life without Luca, if she returned to England, but she thought she was in love with Raphael and he was truly wonderful with Luca. She still wanted to see him. I told her that she could as long as they were very careful and tried to avoid seeing each other when she was with Luca. She moaned that she was always with Luca, and this was true, even when his mother was around and she could not understand how the rich spent so little time with their own children, especially when Luca was such a sweet child. It was then that I told her that Luca was not their child and the whole sorry story that I had been told. She was shocked but said it would explain the lack of love and that it happened a lot in England too, sisters really being mothers, aunts being secret mothers - it had always been the same, to avoid scandal. As long as the child was loved it didn't matter. With Luca though it made her more determined to be there for him and give him that love. I made her promise not to tell anyone and we never discussed it again. She continued to see Raphael but only at night and on her own as she could not risk losing her job and more importantly Luca."

Jasmine, Maddie and Enzo listened, without interruption, until Marietta fell silent. They had a new angle to think about now and discuss later. Marietta could provide no more information than she had already given in her statement thirty years before so they thanked her for the enormous help that she had been to them in revealing her secret and again made the promise to let her know what happened at the end of their investigation.

"Well I wasn't expecting that!" Maddie exclaimed as they returned to their car.

"It is amazing what can come to light, many years after the crime has been committed, when fear is taken away" replied Enzo, sagely. "We see it all the time, sadly. If only we knew these things at the right time the capture of many criminals would be so much easier."

"At least we know now, but we must not see it as the only avenue to explore. Luca's parentage may have nothing to do with his kidnapping. I still prefer the political reason and money. No one seemed to know he was not the Buscolli's biological son and did it really matter?" Jasmine replied.

"Unless Kate told Raphael" Maddie remarked from the backseat of the car.

"Surely that would make asking a ransom for a child that wasn't Marcello's risky?"

Maddie and Enzo nodded in agreement, and they headed off to try and catch Kate's fellow nanny and best friend Lynne Ford, now Signora Russo, at home, if they were lucky.

21

IT was not to be.

Their luck for that day had run out and Signora Rossi was not available any time soon. The maid, answering the imposing door to the Rossi's gated home, informed them that Signor and Signora Rossi were presently at their coastal home in Corsica and would not be back until the following week, if then. They did not like to stay in Milan's stifling heat of summer but came back if Signor Rossi was needed at the office.

Jasmine asked Enzo to request a telephone number for their Corsican home as they needed to speak to Signora Rossi, urgently. The maid left them at the door and went further inside to get it for them after Enzo had shown his police identification.

There was nothing more they could do so they decided to call it a day.

Vincenzo called his son as they were travelling back into the city centre to pass on an invitation from his wife for Jasmine and Maddie to dine with the family again and they gladly accepted. It would be a chance for them all to discuss the new information as well as enjoy a scrumptious meal.

Enzo dropped them off at their apartment and arranged to collect them later in the evening. The two women decided to take a look at the fashion quarter and spend a little money in their unexpected free time and Jasmine hoped that they would be able to speak to Lynne Rossi that evening after their meal.

Dinner was a gloriously lively and chaotic affair with all of the Rappellis present until finally the younger sons were herded off to their rooms to do their homework. Jasmine and Maddie insisted on washing up and then the adults sat down to discuss the day's revelations over a fresh pot of coffee and a plateful of buttered brioche.

At first, Julietta said she would leave them to it but Jasmine said that her opinion would be helpful as an Italian woman's upbringing had probably been very different to her own rather liberal one.

Julietta agreed that her life had certainly taken a more traditional path than her new English friends. She admired their self confidence in taking on what she herself saw as a man's world but it was not for her. "Vincenzo and my sons are my own life's work and that is enough," she remarked, smiling lovingly at her husband.

After Vincenzo and his wife had heard the day's events they both agreed that it was a shock to hear of Luca's parentage, if it was true. None of them held out any real hope of ever finding out either way. Julietta said she understood why it had remained a secret even after the kidnapping and assumed deaths of Luca and Kate, even with such press interest in the story and Marcello Buscolli's high rank.

"It would have been a huge scandal in both Buscolli families, especially in Bari, to have a daughter pregnant out of marriage and to an unsuitable boy. The shame would have been incomparable and the only way forward would be to do exactly what they did do. I think the fact that the child was a boy made all the difference or the girl would have been packed off to a convent and the child adopted by strangers. This way by keeping it literally in the family, there would be no risk of adoptive parents revealing Luca's true identity and Marcello had a male relative disguised as his son to carry on the family name. A girl would not have been as lucrative but, even, so poor Luca did not seem to have the love of adoring parents, did he? At least Kate provided that, if the two maids are to be believed and they never said otherwise at the time."

Vincenza agreed with his wife's observations and added, that he believed that all of the witnesses that they had interviewed at the time were very anxious not to upset the Buscollis in any way, and so had kept any negative thoughts or suspicions at the time to themselves. He was very pleased at their progress, and Jasmine thanked Enzo for helping them gain it with his presence and charm.

Enzo bowed theatrically at the compliment and blew a kiss to Jasmine. His father scowled and advised him to take the matter seriously and Enzo had the grace to blush.

Vincenzo went on to reveal that over the years the police had received many false leads in the case; young men claiming to be Luca; information that was quickly proved to be bogus, on the whereabouts of Kate, all encouraged by the large reward put up by the Buscollis. Finally, the police surmised that if the underworld of the Mafia syndicate could not find any information on what had happened to the child of one of their own, then no one could and the case was set aside with all the other unsolved crimes gathering dust in the nether regions of Italian police stations.

Jasmine suggested that it would be a good time to try and contact Lynne Rossi and asked Vincenzo if he would mind doing so as it would seem more of an official request coming from him. He readily agreed and dialled the number. They all smiled when his mobile phone was quickly answered by Lynne herself.

Vincenzo explained who he was and why he had got in touch and further conversation between the two was conducted in rapid Italian that neither Jasmine nor Maddie could follow sufficiently well, so they had to wait until the call ended to hear what had been said.

"Regrettably, Signora Rossi cannot return to Milan until the end of next week as she and her husband cannot interrupt their holiday for such a minor reason - her words. I explained that you would only be in the country this week as you were very busy people. She said that was your problem not hers and she would be willing to talk to someone else when she returned, but quite what we expected her say that hadn't already been covered thirty years ago, was beyond her. She also declared that wasn't it better to let the dead rest in peace anyway. I suspect this is a witness that you will have trouble getting any positive response from and I would not waste my time delaying your departure to continue your investigation back in England" The summary of his conversation came with a disheartened shrug of Enzo's shoulders.

"Still, Jasmine do not worry. I will look over her original statement if you give me a copy and I will interview her on my own next week. I will then contact you straight away with the information. I confess that I am as eager as you to solve this case that my father could not."

Enzo punched his father lightly on the shoulder to show he meant no harm.

"Careful, regazzo mio" his father chided.

They carried on talking and drinking coffee until Jasmine and Maddie felt they might be outstaying their welcome as Julietta needed to settle her boys down for the night. As they were leaving and saying their goodbyes, Enzo took Jasmine's hand and gently led her away from the others to ask if she would consider going to the opera with him before she left. "La Scala is a sight not to be missed," he said, "and if Maddie does not mind one evening without her, he would greatly enjoy her company."

Jasmine said she would be delighted to go with him and they kissed lightly on both cheeks before joining the others at the door.

Maddie gave her a sly grin and a roll of her eyes as she observed Enzo's wide grin.

Vincenzo smiled at his son. *Like father like son*, he thought having observed the exchange. *La bella regrazzas what they did to your heart.*

22

IT had been agreed that there wasn't anything more to be done in Milan except to drive to the scene of the ransom deaths and to the warehouse where, a few days later, evidence of the abduction had been found after an intensive search of the outskirts of Milan. There were, as now, many abandoned old factory buildings that were ideal to hide out in. A tip off had been handed in from a witness observing unusual activity at the site in the days before the shootings, who only later realised the significance. Vincenzo said that he had booked the morning off to take them himself as he would be retracing his steps from thirty years ago and it might refresh his memory when he saw the place where blood had been discovered. DNA had not yet been an available crime scene resource back then, so they had not been able to glean any real information as to whose blood it was at the time and no one had thought to take a sample. "Different times," he said with a shrug of his shoulders.

Jasmine and Maddie were ready and waiting when Vincenzo arrived at 10.30 the next morning. They had quickly realised that the Italian day tended to start a lot more leisurely than in England. Nothing was to be achieved before a vast amount of coffee drinking it seemed.

As they drove with the hot sun beating down on the car roof they quickly left the affluent parts of Milan and entered first the working-class areas and further on the wasteland of a forgotten industrial past.

After about forty minutes, Vincenzo took a left turn down a beaten track and drove on for a few minutes until they could see an old bridge over a dried-up riverbed.

"This is where the bloodbath took place," Vincenzo solemnly declared. He stopped the car and they got out and took in the fresh air, what there was of it, whilst he recounted what he could remember of that day. It was all in the files but it added a sense of melancholy sadness at the sheer waste of lives the kidnapping had caused for all concerned, all of young men with misplaced ideals that came to nothing in the end and the loss of Kate and Luca forever mourned.

Vincenzo had been one of the many officers arriving at a scene which was etched on his mind forever and being at the site again brought it all back to him. The women respectfully gave him time to gather his emotions together before they all got back in the car to visit the warehouse in silence, all lost in their own thoughts.

Before long they arrived at the derelict site and were disappointed but not entirely surprised to see that there wasn't much left of it. On the few still standing walls someone had sprawled graffiti and skull signs to depict the building's history. It only added to the horror of it all.

The three picked their way gingerly across heaps of fallen bricks and debris until Vincenzo pointed out the spot that had been where Kate and Luca had been kept. The large patch of blood left behind was long gone, covered by years of dust and rain. Vincenzo showed them where there had once been a washroom and a large room that held kitchen items and a large table that now lay crushed in a heap. All evidence of occupation by the gang had been taken away and logged and stored somewhere in the police station but was now lost, as no one had considered that anything could be gained from it. They had retrieved two backpacks, used cups, plates and takeaway boxes and a small selection of toys which had made several of the younger officers tearful as they realised that the little boy who had played with them was more than likely dead now. They had not been able to find any clues to what had become of the rest of the gang, if indeed there were any, or of the two hostages.

It was assumed that at least one gang member must have stayed behind to make sure Kate did not escape, unless, on the other hand, Kate had been part of the abduction all along and wouldn't have been escaping anywhere. There were no leads to suggest what happened either way. It was a dead end that just got harder to solve as the time went by. Although the visit to these two sites hadn't produced any tangible evidence - and hadn't been expected to - Jasmine and Maddie somehow felt an even more urgent desire to find out what had happened to Luca. Had this desolate warehouse for a playground been his last memory? *God*, Jasmine hoped not.

Once again, they returned to the car and drove back to the city centre in silence.

Vincenzo left them to return to work and the two women decided to pay a visit to Il Duomo and whilst sight-seeing in the magnificent building they paused awhile to sit and pray for Luca and Kate and to light candles for them. The day had a sombre feeling that could not be lifted and they spent the evening quietly talking of other matters and then went early to bed. Tomorrow would be their last day in Milan and Jasmine would be spending the evening at La Scala with Enzo which surprisingly, as she didn't do dates, she was eagerly anticipating. It would be a wonderful way to clear her head from the sadness this case was causing her.

She knew from experience, that in order to help the families of missing people, the investigator must not get so emotionally involved that vital clues were missed because it was too painful to look for them clearly.

Her team back home would now do everything they possibly could to give Santa Buscolli the answers she was paying them for and deal with their own emotions later.

Hopefully this willingness would continue and whilst, sadly, neither women felt it likely that Kate and Luca were alive at least they were more confident of giving Santa Buscolli closure.

24

BACK at the Brite Agency office the team were gathered around Jasmine's desk discussing the evidence the two women had gathered and how best to go forward here in England with the case. Jasmine informed them that she would be going straightaway to give Santa her report on their progress in Milan and that she wanted Evie to interview Kate's mother as she would be better at this as a former policewoman and also, having a child herself. Evie agreed that she thought this a good idea and she would be able to organise someone to look after her own daughter, Freya, easily enough.

Jasmine asked Hugo to find out where Mrs. Marshall was now living and any other information on Kate's family that might be useful. Caro and Maddie were to continue tackling the agency's current workload for the moment. It didn't take long for Hugo to obtain Mrs. Marshall's telephone number because she had continued to live at the same address as she had been at in 1978, Kate's childhood home. He handed it over to Evie who got her notepad ready and dialled the number.

It rang briefly and was answered by and elderly voice, "Hello, June Marshall speaking. Who's calling?"

"Good morning, Mrs. Marshall. I wonder if you have a moment to speak to me about the disappearance of your daughter Kate in 1978. My name is Evie Baxter and I work for the Brite Missing Persons Agency. We've has been asked to re-open the case on your daughter and Luca Buscolli. I would be grateful if I could arrange to come and see you as soon as possible."

"Have you found them?" June Marshall almost shrieked in shock that reverberated down the telephone line to Evie.

"No, no, Mrs. Marshall. I am sorry to have given you false hope. No, I would just like to speak to you about what happened at the time and to see if you have any fresh memories that might help in our enquiries."

"I do not wish to talk to anyone about the loss of my Kate and how she was portrayed. It was thirty years ago. Let us all rest in peace. Goodbye, Miss. Baxter." That was the abrupt answer as the phone was put down on Evie.

"Well that went well!" Evie called over to Hugo and Jasmine.

Far away, on the other end of the line, June Marshall sank to the hall floor. *Oh my God, oh my God, after thirty years my sins have finally come home to roost*, she realised, beginning to weep silently.

"Let's give her some time to process the information and then try again in a few hours, Evie. We really need her help, if we are to progress, as Kate's side of the story hasn't really been told in any great detail. We need to know how her family coped with the loss and the accusation that their daughter was involved in the kidnapping. Mrs. Marshall doesn't live all that far from here so try to get her to see you at the latest tomorrow, will you?"

"Sure, Jasmine, I'll try my best."

"I'm off to see Santa now so keep me informed. Bye you two, Hugo don't play on the computer all day. Do something useful."

"Always do sis, always do. You just don't appreciate me" Hugo replied, indignantly.

Meanwhile, June Marshall had had time to pull herself together and taken a strong glass of gin and tonic to calm her nerves. She had called her elder sister who had advised her to think straight and welcome the investigator into her home which would be the normal reaction of a grieving mother. After all, any resumption of the search for her missing daughter ought to be welcomed and grasped with both hands. "Play it by ear," she advised, "and then call her back later, and above all stay calm."

So, when Evie rang again June apologised for her abruptness, blaming the shock, and agreed that Evie should come to her home that evening. Evie was surprised at the quick turnaround but pleased and set about arranging a babysitter for her four-year-old daughter.

June Marshall lived in a quiet suburban, mainly working-class area near Birmingham that was about an hour on the motorway from The Brite Agency office, so she could easily get there and back before Freya's bedtime. Being a single parent, she tried to ensure she was always there to kiss her goodnight and tell her how precious she was.

At five o'clock she was standing at the front door of a pleasant semi-detached, three bedroomed house that looked well cared for and the door was opened by a tall, slim woman in her sixties with a distinct similarity to her young daughter, Kate, from the photographs that Evie had seen.

June introduced herself and welcomed her into a spacious living room where she had set out a tea tray with tea, coffee and biscuits for her guest.

Evie thanked her profusely for allowing her to talk to her and insisted that she only wanted to form a more detailed impression of a much-loved daughter, rather than a suspect or victim of violence.

June poured them tea and settled into the chair opposite Evie and replied that she wanted to do anything to help, that might shed some light on what happened, but it was so long ago, that she feared her daughter was gone forever along with the poor child.

"Well, Mrs. Marshall, it would be helpful if you could describe in your own words what happened in May 1978 from your perspective starting with when you were first contacted about the kidnapping."

"Ok, I will try my best to remember that terrible time."

She took a few moments to finish her tea and replace the cup onto the tray. She placed her hands in her lap, absent-mindedly wringing a handkerchief and began. "Back then, we relied on letters to hear from each other. Some arrived, some didn't. The Italian Postal service was continuously interrupted by strikes. The Italians would strike for almost any reason, it seemed. It was a great worry to me and international phone calls were very expensive. I worried so much about her being over there all alone, but I never in my wildest fears would have imagined that I would lose her from a kidnapping and find she was being portrayed in the Italian media as some kind of monster. I was hounded by the newspapers for a story but I refused to feed their frenzy. I just wanted my daughter back safely. She had written to me that she was loving living in Milan and had friends and a boyfriend, although she complained of not having enough free time, as she pretty much looked after the child, Luca, all the time. Kate had been used to going out frequently at home and she found this hard but recognised that Italian women were not given much freedom to run around the city unaccompanied. She had a best friend called Lynne and a young man called Raphael that she went around with, mainly. She said how much she had come to love Luca and assured me that the Buscolli family treated her very well and as part of their family not as an employee. She also said that they were a very well-respected family in Milan but she never informed me of Marcello Buscolli's status. I would have been much more worried if she had, knowing how involved the mafia was in all that business that went

believed herself to be in love with the Italian boy and was very happy. She adored Luca and was very attached to him and took great delight in every new word of English that he pronounced in his working-class accent. To this day, she would not believe that her friend could have harmed that boy or had anything to do with the kidnapping. Kate had simply been a young, naïve girl just like herself and had had no interest in anything around her but having the time of her life before returning to her rather mundane life back in England.

Lynne had worked hard at dis-engaging herself from the crime back then and having lost her job as a nanny due to her association with Kate she had gone to Milan University, funded by her parents and working very hard in a restaurant for three years, ending up teaching English in an infant school, until meeting her husband and becoming a housewife and mother. She did not want the life she had created for herself disturbed and knowing her husband so well, she knew he would not forgive her omission of not admitting to her part in a crime that had been the talk of Milan for many years after all hope of Kate and Luca being alive, was gone.

When she had read through her statement and refreshed her memory she handed it back to Enzo.

"Once again, I can only say that I have nothing more to add. I got on with my life and tried to forget that I knew of the kidnappers, at least Raphael. I cannot say whether Davido was involved but I'm sure he would have been thoroughly investigated at the time and I don't recall his name being mentioned in the papers. I would have noticed."

"I'm sorry, who are you talking about? Let me look at your statement again. Davido? Davido who? Ah yes, here you say how you met him the day Kate met Raphael. I don't seem to have read his statement but of course you are right - he would have been a person of great importance to the investigation. See, Lynne, you have indeed been a great help as I must look into this immediately. I don't suppose you remember his surname, do you?"

"I am sorry, I do not. I really had nothing to do with him so I did not know it or Raphael's. I am not sure whether Kate even knew their names. That was how it was in the seventies. We were naïve and stupid and trusted everyone. Nothing bad was ever going to happen to us. How wrong we were. I am sure you will have his statement somewhere, as the police knew of him. It has probably gotten lost or filed wrongly. After all it was thirty years ago. I'm surprised you've still got any of the paperwork."

"A case is never closed, Signora, until we solve it. Thank you again for your time and I can assure you that we will not bother you again, unless you would like to know the outcome of the investigation?"

"If you find them alive, yes. If not, then let them rest in peace. Goodbye Signor Rappelli."

With that she shook his hand and left the café. Enzo paid the bill and scurried over to the station opposite to ask his father what had become of this Davido's statement. How could such an important document not be in the file?

Fortunately, his father was in his office alone.

"Papa, I have just interviewed Signora Lynne Rossi. She had nothing to add but she mentioned the friend of Kate's boyfriend, Raphael Grecco. She pointed out that she had told the police of his existence and that he, most certainly, would have been interviewed, even seen as a suspect in the kidnapping. So where is his statement?"

His father looked at his son and considered what he had just said. "This is indeed news to me, son. It seems that the cold case is in need of careful inspection. Of course, this Davido would have been of enormous interest to us. The statement is not in the file which is strange but can be put down to human error. As you know, every time the evidence box is taken out of the archives and looked at, it is always signed for and resealed afterwards. All statements, evidence, photographs of the scene, fingerprints and police write-ups are in there and of course anything that might well contain DNA. I will get onto my sergeant immediately to go down to the archive department and find out who has taken it out over the years and how the hell a piece of evidence has somehow gone missing." There was anger in his voice now. "Incompetent fools; heads will roll for this. How foolish we will look to Jasmine Brite and her colleagues."

Enzo agreed, silently, and left his father to calm down.

26

OFFICER *Verdi went down to the basement that housed all the police files on record. The station was in the process of transferring all paperwork on to the vast computer files, listing current, closed and open cases, but it was a time-consuming task so open, what were commonly called cold, cases would be the last to be processed. These were in a room of their own occupied by a receptionist who kept track of their coming and goings. This was the most boring of jobs so the desk was manned by several part-time civilian staff who had been former police officers but still liked to keep their hands in by taking out the odd cold case and studying it with a fresh pair of eyes. Sometimes it worked but most of the time it didn't. Ispettore Rappelli had requested that the Buscolli File was to be brought to him immediately with a list of who had taken it out in the last thirty years, which reception would have recorded. Signing it out was straight forward and sitting quietly at the table for such purpose, it was a simple task to pick up the top sheet in the file box containing the list of officers, their signatures and the signature of the officer on reception at the time. Ispettore Rappelli, himself, was the last person on the list and there had been only a few in the thirty years who had taken it out, probably the retired officers who worked in the cold case room. The only person that had taken out the evidence box who needed to be taken off that list was sitting looking at it. It had been taken out over twenty years ago and studied, when a young police recruit had obtained it to see what it contained and having seen the damning evidence about a boy called Davido Romano, a suspect who could not be found after his initial statement, and no longer existed under that name, took the statement and details of the said boy and destroyed them. Self-preservation was vital and it was time to get involved in this re-opened case to ensure it did not come to a positive conclusion.*

Officer Verdi's life depended upon it.

27
The hideout, 11th May 1978

KATE rushed to Luca's side and cradled him in her arms to shield his eyes from the terrible sight. Davido was crouched down beside Carla's prone body, desperately trying to give her the kiss of life, whilst Stefana ran to find something to stem the flow of blood seeping out of her friend. When she returned, she gently pulled Davido away and held him. There was to be no reprieve for Carla She was dead, her life drained quickly away as a result of a single shot to the heart, a shot Stefana herself had fired in the confusion.

Kate had quietened the frightened child and stepped outside, away from the drama in complete shock. What will happen now? she wondered.

"Davido, caro mio. I have destroyed us and am a murderer. What are we to do? How the hell do we get out of this? Carla! Carla! My friend, why did you make me do it? My God! We are all lost."

Stefana broke into loud sobs.

Davido sat comforting his girlfriend, silently and calmly taking charge of the situation and devising a plan that might just work. He came from a world away from the wealthy Milanese life, a poor fishing family working near the docks of the port of Genoa. One of seven brothers, he had been the only one who had been allowed to go to university after completing his national service which all young men had to do for two years. He had been proud to serve his country and it have given him a life far removed from the stinking, impoverished life aboard the fishing trawlers and low life that occupied his home town. He returned with a hunger for a different life and had been well on the way as a gifted student until he had been introduced to Raphael Grecco and his influential friends. Now he would have to return to that fishing town and seek out those old playmates who had stayed put and lived on the edge of criminality, just to make a living. He would have to eat humble pie - Davido the conquering hero, felled by trying to be someone he was not. He was no better than the boys he had left behind; he was much worse, a kidnapper of children and a murderer. How ironic and how he would break his family's heart. Now, he must again become the boy that ran with the crowd, barefoot and feral and at home amongst the sailors, prostitutes and drunkards who littered the port and he must disappear.

"Calm yourself caro mio. I will get us out of this. Go and get Kate. I will explain what we need to do. I will soon be identified as Raphael's friend but you are not connected in any way, so go about your business as usual. When this is all over we will be together again without suspicion, however long that takes so we must be strong. Firstly, you must go quickly and buy brunette hair dye, scissors, clothes for a girl the same size as Luca and bring some of your clothes for Kate. You're about the same size, aren't you? We must disguise them in order to get to Genoa, where I will hide them. You must not panic, Stefana. Please pull yourself together. We cannot change what has happened and remember that Carla was volatile and she held the gun not you. She intended to kill Kate, I'm sure of it but her death was an accident, caro, an accident."

He kissed her, gently, and gradually she became calmer and understanding that there was a way out for them, she got up and went to fetch Kate and Luca. They must now explain the plan to Kate and convince her she needed to cooperate since unfortunately returning herself and Luca was no longer an option for any of them. It was an unholy mess but if they stuck together there was a way out, and she trusted Davido implicitly.

Kate refused to bring Luca back into the room containing Carla's corpse, so Davido and Stefana sat outside in the blazing heat and discussed the plan. Kate was in shock and numbly agreed to anything that would get her and Luca out of there as fast as possible. She would think about the implications of Carla's death later when she could cope - if she could cope. The last few days had brought her mind to breaking point and the need to keep calm for Luca's sake, at least in appearance, had taken its toll.

Stefana left quickly, instructing Kate to take Luca into the old shed that had been used as a temporary cell for them whilst the kidnappers were away. It was warm and now that there was no need to lock them in the window could be left open to let in air and Luca was happy to play with his meagre toys in there.

Meanwhile Davido cleaned up the evidence of the shooting. He wrapped Carla in an old blanket Kate had been using, said a prayer over her for her soul, and then picked her up over his shoulder and laid her gently on the ground outside the hideout, until he had a place

28

IT was just getting light when Davido took the turning for Genoa, which consisted of the upper town and a portside, lower town. The whole region was built between mountainous areas and was reached by almost impossible roads to navigate, many passing through tunnels built under the houses and pedestrians must by necessity find their way through narrow alleys and tiny precarious streets that, although charming to the average tourist, were confusing to all but Genoese natives. With the added chaos of a tourist spot in mid-season and a bustling major commercial port, Davido surmised that Kate and Luca would be well hidden in his home town.

As Kate gazed out of the window she was mesmerised by its outstanding beauty. How she wished she could have seen it in different circumstances. Now she was fighting for her future through no fault of her own except her naivety and youth. Davido threaded his way through the streets until he reached a more impoverished area near the port where tourists were few and the Genoese people earned their living, crowded together in cottages not unlike the ones to be found in most fishing ports in Europe. Davido was home.

He stopped the car at the small parking area allocated to dock workers from the busy port. He would have to find a better place to park but it would do for the moment. He picked Luca up into his arms and Kate followed him through the maze of alleyways and cobbled streets which were barely wide enough to walk through. She felt as though she had slipped through a hole in time and landed in a medieval town and it all added to her feeling of unreality. Genoa seemed unchanged except for the tourists who had lifted its citizens out of their impoverished fishing heritage. It was truly beautiful.

Within minutes they came to a small alley that led to a what appeared to be a dilapidated frontage of a small cottage, comprising a faded door and tiny window squeezed into the wall. Davido told her not to speak, to stay calm and let him explain to his family what they were doing on their doorstep. He rapped loudly on the ancient knocker. Seconds later the door was swung open by a middle-aged woman. "Chi e la?"

"Valentina, it is I, Davido, Buon giorno mia sorella."

"Mamma mia, Davido!" she exclaimed, grabbing him into a bearhug and raining kisses all over his face before she had even noticed he was not alone. When his sister-in-law had finally got over her shock he stepped back and drew Kate, who was holding Luca, forward and introduced them.

"Valentina, please excuse the unexpectedness of our visit but our cause is urgent. This is Anna and her daughter Lola, my very good friend from university. Please invite us in and I will explain."

"Of course. Of course, come in, this is your home. You are a silly boy; you do not need an invite, imagine!" She cuffed him gently on the ear and ushered them inside.

Beyond the front door was a surprise to Kate as it opened onto a long, wide hall leading to several small rooms that seemed to have been tacked on at various stages of the old cottage's history. They passed through two rooms used for general living, then a little study that contained a narrow staircase leading up to the first level and a doorway into a vast kitchen that seemed to be built out of the actual mountain rock. This room was obviously the hubbub of family life and four men sat at a kitchen table eating a hearty breakfast. They glanced up from their plates as Valentina presented the three new arrivals and at once, a cacophony of male voices rang out greeting Davido like the long-lost son, which in many ways he was.

Kate could not follow the rapid Genoese dialect, so she stood waiting to be introduced to the rest of the family and Luca looked on in confusion. *The poor child must be wondering who on earth all these new adults were that he's been surrounded by, these last few days,* she thought. He had only mentioned Mama and Santa a few times and Papa not at all and she had quickly distracted him. He was, after all, used to being with Kate all the time.

Valentina ushered Kate to a large settee taking up the far wall of the room and offered her a cup of coffee and fruitcake that was in pride of place on the breakfast table. Kate accepted them, gratefully as she was very hungry. She sat Luca down beside her and Valentina gave him a slice of toast and cup of orange juice. She attempted to engage Luca in conversation, calling him a *bella bambina*, beautiful little girl, but he ignored her and nestled his head into Kate's side.

"Ah, pouvre bambina, she is confused by so many strangers, I think," said Valentina, in halting English. "Scusa Anna, I do not speak the English well. We will have to speak Italian, I am afraid, very slowly," she said, with a smile.

"Do not worry Signora Romano, I am sorry to impose on you like this. I must leave it to Davido to explain my circumstances to you and your family," Kate replied in Italian.

As she sat and ate with Luca, Davido quickly explained what they were doing there, to his family. He told them that *Anna* was a fellow student and had been in an abusive relationship with Lola's father who was also a foreigner. He didn't enlighten them any further but was anxious not to say he was Italian, fearing that they would be reluctant to help the English girl take the child away from an Italian national. Davido said he had helped her get away and had come to Genoa in the hope of getting a captain of a trawler bound for England to take Kate home to her family.

The Romanos sat silently listening, asking a few questions, until seemingly satisfied, the eldest man, presumably their father, got up from the table and approached Kate and patted on the shoulder. "You are most welcome in my humble home. My daughter-in-law, Valentina will make you comfortable, you and the little one, and my sons will see how we can help you," he said, in his broad Genoese, which Davido translated for him.

Kate nodded and thanked him.

Davido then introduced her to his father and brothers, "This, of course is my father Alfredo, then Fredo who is the husband of Valentina, who looks after us all like a mama." He planted a kiss on Valentina's cheek and she blushed and ushered him away.

"Next, is Alfonzo, Antonio and Roberto. My two other brothers are married and live nearby with their wives and children. They are Angelo and Dante. You can see Mama and Papa were very fortunate in having so many sons to carry on the family name," he said, with a chuckle and a wink at his father. In the car on their journey throughout the night, he had already spoken of his mother's death, some years before.

Valentina quickly got food for the tired travellers and told the men to make haste so that they could sit around the table. The men went quickly about their business and were soon out of the door and off to work at the docks.

Valentina and Davido talked rapidly, catching up on gossip and general conversation whilst Kate encouraged Luca to eat. Then

Valentina showed Kate and Luca to a little room that she said had been Davido's when he came home but he would sleep with his brother Robert instead. Davido, who had accompanied them so he could translate, said that would not be necessary as after he had had a good rest he would be returning to Milan as he could not take time off his study at university. He said, "I am entrusting Anna and Lola into your care until I return."

Valentina said, "Of course they are most welcome and I will enjoy having a woman's company around the house for a change and having a little girl to cherish is a bonus."

Kate thanked her profusely and said, "I will try my best to help and not get in the way and hopefully my stay will not need to be a long one as I'm eager to go home to my family."

Valentina gave her a squeeze in sympathy and left the three of them to talk whilst she cleared up breakfast.

"Kate, please do not worry. You are very safe here and my family are good people. They accept our story and as long as you stay as Anna and Lola they will not suspect a thing. It is for their safety too that they do not know who you are. We do not want to bring the police down on them for any reason. However, if the police put out a reward for information, this is a small community and I could not trust that the money would not be tempting. Go out as little as possible as the neighbours will be curious. Of course, talk to Valentina and become friends but never forget you are Anna and above all do not let anyone find out that Lola is in fact a boy. I will return at the weekend and we can get things underway. I will know how much the police know of Raphael's friends and what has happened since their deaths. Do not be tempted to look at a paper or talk at all about the kidnapping even if my family comment. I am sorry I have to leave you alone but it is the only way." Davido ended with a heavy sigh.

"Thank you Davido for what you're doing for me. You could have just left me somewhere and taken your chances that I would not be able to identify you and Stefana and be left accused of being part of the whole nightmare. You are a good man and I believe you and Stefana were caught up in something you couldn't get out of. I do not believe you would have wanted to kidnap an innocent child. We are all victims now. I pray that you will be rid of me very soon and that I will return to England somehow and that you will return Luca to his parents."

"God willing. Now let us rest and then I will be off."

Kate tried to settle Luca down but he was over-excited so she washed and changed him and joined Valentina downstairs in her garden where Luca played happily with his toys. Valentina had busied herself about the house and found out some old toys for Luca and then announced that she was off to the market and wouldn't be long so Anna was to make herself at home.

It was the first time Kate had been truly alone since the day of the kidnap and it gave her time to take in all that had happened. If they managed to pull this off, life would never be the same again for any of them. Perhaps Luca would be the least affected she hoped, but he would be forever the boy who was kidnapped. Kate, however - what would become of her when she reached England? She could not go to her mother as the police would be waiting to see if she contacted her family so where would she go? Here she sat with Luca playing by her feet in a glorious Mediterranean garden as if she hadn't a care in the world when nothing could be further from the truth. She wished, with all her heart, that her mother was beside her at that moment to hold her close and whisper that everything would be alright but she knew that it would never be alright ever again.

Gazing down at the little boy she loved so much, she wiped a silent tear from her eye and tried her best to block out her terrible misgivings and concentrate on the innocent child and keeping him safe, as was her job.

29

DAVIDO left after lunch, having explained to his family, who had returned to eat and rest, as was the custom in the heat of summer in most cities in Italy, to return to work when the midday sun had cooled somewhat, that *Anna* was able to understand them if they spoke slowly but was not a confident speaker of Italian and not to take offence if she seemed quiet. He said that he would be back Saturday morning and would like his brothers' help in arranging passage on one of the trawlers for Anna and her daughter as soon as possible. The men agreed that they would ask around.

Only Fredo seemed a little reluctant and had frequently glanced, thoughtfully, at Kate since their arrival at his home.

Valentina, his wife, had on the other hand embraced the strangers and had been trying desperately to engage *Lola*, la piccolo bambina, despite Luca's indifference to anyone but Kate. Her daughter was shy in the company of adults, professed Kate, and would come to Valentina gradually.

Secretly, this was a worry to Kate as she could not predict how Luca would react to any situation and of course he would not answer to the name of *Lola* anyway. Stefana had provided play clothes in girlish colours and Luca was too young to have a preference and dressed as a girl he looked like a girl with his cherubic baby fat. Luckily, his speech was that of an eighteen-month-old toddler with incomplete sentences and besides he used only English when speaking to Kate as part of her job had been to ensure that Luca was brought up bi-lingual, speaking Italian to his family and English to her, which he did with surprising ease.

The rest of the day went by without incident as Kate helped around the house and prepared the main meal that would be eaten in the evening when the men had returned.

Luca was put to bed before they arrived back and the evening was spent pleasantly out in the garden in the evening sunshine, the men playing cards and the two women just resting after clearing away the meal. Kate had survived her first day with these strangers and hoped that this would continue if she made herself useful and did not have to answer too many inquisitive questions from Valentina, who

holding the victims would, if they had any sense, give themselves up or at least return Kate and Luca to the family or to the police. A phone number was printed for anyone with information to call.

Davido had sighed, knowing it would not be long before the police would come calling to interrogate him. He must be prepared. He quickly dumped the newspaper in the bin and left the university, taking the metro out of the city to plan his next move. He had had the sense to carry with him everything he might need from his apartment so that he would not have to return there if he was identified quickly. His best bet was to stay out of town in the youth hostel until he could return to Genoa. He desperately wanted to contact Stefana and see how she was coping but knew he could not. It was better for her if she not know of his whereabouts. He felt totally alone, the success of the end to this nightmare depending solely on him, or the lives of an innocent girl would have been blighted forever by him and his stupidity in getting involved with Raphael, who he had foolishly hero-worshipped. All he could now was to try and repair some of the damage and get Kate to England and Luca home.

He had stayed at the hostel, keeping himself to himself, and then caught the train to Genoa, not wanting to risk being stopped on entry to the autostrada in Milan. He could travel anonymously by rail.

So here he was back in Genoa with Kate where they must find passage for her as quickly as possible.

Kate listened silently, wondering what her own family were thinking of the kidnap. Were her mother and father in Milan? How she wanted to fly to their sides.

Davido took hold of hand and said, "I'm so sorry for what I did."

Kate could not answer him as the unshed tears threatened to choke her. She could not find it in her heart to give him any comfort; after all he was one of her kidnappers, a fact she could not forgive, whichever way he intended to make amends now.

Luca stirred and they got up from the bench and returned to the Romano home.

Valentina was busy preparing a feast for the whole family was dining al fresco out in the garden that evening. Kate would meet Angelo, Dante and their wives and children and she was anxious in case the children discovered Luca would not answer to the name *Lola*. Children were, after all, very astute. She would have to deal with that if it arose. She could not put him to bed to miss such a family occasion - Valentina would be offended.

Dinner at the Romanos *en masse* was a sight to behold. They seemed to pour out of the kitchen and spread all over the garden, which was not large by any account. Children vied for space to breathe away from the adults who were busy chattering away, nineteen to the dozen, whilst their offspring darted in and out of their legs chasing each other. In the midst of the chaos was a sumptuous meal laid out on a large wooden table. The evening sun was at its glorious best and a gentle breeze blew, cooling their hot bodies down. Kate was used to scenes such as this with the Buscolli family who spent most weekends dining out in the courtyard of an old farmhouse and farm on the outskirts of Milan. All Italians loved to get away from the stifling heat of the city if they could possibly do so.

Davido mingled between all of his relatives, letting them catch up on his life in Milan but he careful to keep Kate close to him so that she didn't feel overwhelmed. Meanwhile *Lola* played happily with the nieces and nephews who were excited to have a new playmate amongst them.

As the evening progressed, the noise settled down and the men sat around the cleared table playing cards whilst the Romano women sat with Kate, keeping an eye on their tired children. Antonio's wife, Gulia, had constantly tried to engage Kate in conversation throughout the meal, speaking slowly so that Kate could follow her heavy Genoese dialect. She had wanted to know when *Anna* had arrived in Italy? Was she married? What had she been studying at Davido's university that they had had an opportunity to meet? Of course, Kate did not know what Davido was studying and so avoided answering. Would *Lola's* father come looking for her? What about his family? Where was he from? The questions were endless and Kate tried her best to fabricate answers that would satisfy Gulia and the others, who were listening with interest. Davido had tried to rescue her but did not want to appear too wary of *Anna* answering for herself. Valentina eventually told them to leave the poor girl alone and seeing that *Lola* was fast asleep on *Anna's* lap, suggested that her sisters-in-law should gather up the children and their husbands and bid everyone goodbye.

Finally, the men ended their game and the two married brothers agreed to leave saying that they had all got to get up early for work in the morning. By then Kate had already retired with Luca, thanking Valentina for a wonderful evening, leaving Davido and his father and two remaining brothers to talk amongst themselves and enjoy a few more bottles of wine.

Early the next morning Luca awoke up raring to go so Kate washed and dressed him, anxiously hoping Valentina would not burst into the bedroom and discover *Lola* was a boy. When they were ready, they went downstairs and joined Valentina in the kitchen to help with breakfast.

Once again, all the men had returned from work at the docks for a hearty meal before continuing their morning shift. Davido was sitting with them, looking pre-occupied as he glanced up at Kate as she entered the room. There was a strange, unusually sombre atmosphere in the large kitchen. Kate noticed it at once. She bid everyone a good morning and sat Luca down in a highchair that, once again, Valentina had provided and let him feed himself from the plentiful array of food in front of him.

"Anna, buon giorno," said Alfredo. "Please sit down." He beckoned her to the empty seat beside Davido, who looked deeply concerned at Kate. Something was seriously up, she surmised.

"Anna, or should I say, Kate," Davido began. "My family know who you are. I am so sorry." He then quietly explained that Gulia had seen the Milanese newspapers and they had been running a picture of Kate, albeit a younger version of her, probably obtained from her parents, and a recent picture of Luca. Gulia had recognised them, immediately, last evening and told her husband when they got home, who then informed his father straight away.

When the rest of the family had been told they confronted Davido demanding to know the truth. He had broken down and revealed all to his heartbroken family who now had a kidnapper in their midst.

Kate gasped at this news and looked at them all in horror.

Davido took hold of her hand whilst Alfredo waved his hands in the air saying, "Prego, prego, please, Kate, do not be alarmed, child. Davido continue, prego."

Davido explained that he had admitted that Kate and Luca had been kidnapped for ransom by Raphael Grecco's comrades who supported Brigate Rosse and he himself had been persuaded to be one of them. As the papers had revealed, most of them had been killed in the shootout when the handover went wrong. He had gone on to reveal to his family what had happened to Carla and how sorry he was for his part in it all. He had begged them to help him get Kate to England as soon as possible and then promised he would return Luca to his family. He had lied to them all so that they would not have to be part of his terrible crime, he pleaded.

His father and brothers had angrily chastised him but after exhausting all their condemnation, had said that of course they would help and protect him, because he was family.

Kate interrupted Davido to apologise to his family for coming to their home. She said, "I was frightened of being accused of being part of the kidnapping because Raphael was my boyfriend. I was afraid no one would believe I was innocent and that I'd be lost in prison, where no one could help me."

Alfredo told her to stop. "You have nothing, nothing to be sorry for, my child. It is I who is deeply ashamed of my son and will not stop until he has righted his crime and at least returned you and lo bambino, Luca to his parents." He was speaking in slow, careful Italian so that Kate might understand how deeply upset he was and Davido could only look down at the floor, shame-facedly.

Alfredo continued, informing Kate, "The family has talked, long into the night and decided it would be safer for them all if Kate and Luca, still disguised as *Anna* and *Lola*, stayed down by the dock area until passage on a trawler can be secured. Fredo has gone out to call on Antonio and Gulia and had let them in on the situation and to ensure they do not tell anyone what they have discovered, as there is a hefty reward being offered by the Buscollis for any information. If Kate and Luca can stay hidden until they are gone from Genoa ,no one will be any the wiser."

Davido muttered that his family were no fans of authority anyway and had their own secrets.

His brother, Roberto, butted in. "At least none of us are kidnappers and disposers of bodies. Davido has out done us all."

Their father angrily told him to be quiet. "It does not help and we will deal with Davido in our own way when the crisis is over if he gets away with it."

Davido pointed out that his brothers had already found an apartment for them to stay in owned by a fellow worker and used only by his family when they visited him in the summer months. "I will take them there now and then return immediately to Milan where I will, most certainly, be interviewed by the police."

Once again, Alfredo apologised to Kate for his son's actions and then asked that God would find it in his mercy to forgive them all their sins even though he himself would find it hard to forgive his son for kidnapping an innocent child.

Davido hung his head in shame.

But they now had a way forward.

30

KATE and Luca had been in the tiny, dark and dirty apartment, little more than a bedsit really, for three days. There had been no word from Davido and Kate was beside herself with worry. He had said that he would get in touch with his father if he could possibly do so but there had been no word. Kate and the family could only suspect that he was being held for questioning by the police and unable to contact the family.

Luca was increasingly fractious at being cooped up in the tiny space and the heat was unbearable. Kate wondered if the child was beginning to understand that something was very wrong about their situation. Who knew what young children remembered or picked up from adults? She was worried that his crying would draw unwanted attention from the neighbours and decided, although she had been expressly told not to leave the apartment, to take him for a walk and some much-needed fresh air. She dressed him in girl's clothes and let them out of the apartment into the hot summer sun. Valentina had kept the pushchair so she would have to walk slowly and probably carry him back but it was worth it to be outside again.

The dockside area was vastly different from the upper town and local tourist attractions, although it still had its share of ancient churches, she noticed. Its main attraction for tourists, however, was the famous Palazzo which instead of standing in grounds worthy of its ancient history, stood in between a busy road, a railway and the fast moving, noisy motorway above it. All this was a distraction from its undeniable beauty.

There were other, lesser attractions, down in the Lower town and the port. A medieval arcade ran parallel to the pier. It was, however, filled with trashy tourist mementos, second-hand imported junk and an array of fish stalls, as was to be expected on the enormous portside. The saving grace was the Church of San Giovanni de Pre with its beautiful bell tower and the sight of the great ships coming into port. There was also the lighthouse to admire but even so most tourists would fare better spending their time in High Town.

For Kate, Lower Town was fine. She wandered around trying to look inconspicuous and, happily, Luca was laughing and enjoying watching the fishermen and boats who called a greeting to the *little girl.* He was fascinated by the enormous ocean liners docked for the day. Luckily, there were enough people around for Kate and Luca to go about unnoticed. Kate bought ice-creams for them both and cooling drinks and they sat watching the world go by.

As midday approached and the Genoese made their way indoors to escape the worst of the heat, Kate decided to visit the Church and sit inside its cool walls, and, she thought, perhaps to say a few prayers for her safe passage home. Luca was tired so she hoped he would fall asleep in the coolness of the silent, *Holy* place.

As she entered, she felt an instant calmness that she had not felt since the day of the kidnapping, since meeting Raphael outside another beautiful building, Il Duomo, recognising the irony of the fact. There were a few old women dressed in black with their heads covered inside but they did not look up from their prayers. Kate lay Luca down on a bench, using a kneeling pad for a pillow. He was already instantly and soundly asleep in her arms. She sat beside him and began to pray.

Lost in thought, unsure how long she had been sitting there, Kate was startled to find the Chaplain at her side.

She had been silently praying and reflecting on how much she would miss the little boy, sleeping innocently by her side, and also her life in Milan. She would not have chosen to return to England so soon, perhaps never, for she truly loved Italy, its people and their way of life. She might sometimes have missed her parents and got homesick but she had grown up a lonely, only child whose parents had worked full-time and left her to her own devices. She loved them, of course, but sadly didn't feel close to them and she had been shy and found it hard to make friends. Italy had been a new start for her and as she loved the company of children, having earned pocket money babysitting for friends and neighbours she felt she would be suited to a nanny post. The first time she had felt unadulterated love for someone was for this little boy. She could not have loved him more if he had been her own child, she had come to realise. It would be hard to say goodbye and she was sad that he would probably forget her very soon, a distant memory of his baby years.

"Buon pomeriggio, Signora. You are seeking God's blessing or merely escaping the afternoon sun maybe?" he said with a smile. "You could not find a more beautiful place to do so, do you not agree?"

"Both, Father. I hope I am not intruding or doing anything wrong? My daughter fell asleep and we needed to rest." Kate replied in Italian.

"No, no, Signora. I make the amusement. You are Englese, si? You speak Milanese with the accent of the English. You are on vacation, maybe? La bambina has the best idea, si?" He smiled down at the sleeping child, whilst Kate answered his barrage of questions, agreeing that she was, indeed, on holiday but lived in Milan.

The priest was quite young, she was surprised to see; no more than in his late twenties, she surmised. How fortunate he was to have this magnificent church in his charge but she knew that many young Catholic men entered the church straight from school with the blessing and pride of their families in Italy.

"You look troubled, Signora. Would you like to talk or should I leave you to your quiet contemplation?"

"I am fine, Father. I am just very hot, but thank you for your concern."

Although, there was nothing she wanted more than to confide in this gentleman of God, she knew that she must not give in to the desire. She was anxious in case Luca awoke and called her Kate or that she gave something else away.

The priest nodded in assent and walked away saying, "Enjoy your holiday. God's blessing to you and your daughter."

Luca slept on for a while and Kate walked around the church, gazing at the painting and statues that adorned every available space. The magnificence of the altar was a sight to behold and it always amazed Kate that the poorest communities seemed to have the most extravagant demonstrations of their worship of God. *Surely, He could not need this wealth at the expense of his people's poverty*, she thought, sceptically.

Luca awoke lively and hungry and in need of a nappy change so she made her way down to the port again and found a little shop selling all she needed. As she went to pay for her purchases, engaging in polite conversation with the shop owner, Luca let go of her hand and made a dash for the outside.

"Luca! Come back!" she shouted, in panic, realising, too late, what she'd done.

The whole family were present as Alfredo rang Davido who answered straight away and they spoke for a few minutes, the rest of the family nodding away at whatever Alfredo was saying to his son.

Then he beckoned Kate over to the phone.

"Kate, Kate how are you holding up?" Davido asked, anxiously. "I am so sorry. I hope you know that. If I could go back in time I would. I have ruined your life. You were happy here. I will never forgive myself. Luca will forget but you and I will not."

"It can't be undone, Davido, but we can only hope that I get home to my family eventually, and that Luca does indeed forget all of this, although sadly that means he will forget all about me too. You realise, of course, I cannot just return to my parents. The police will be looking for me," she said, forlornly. She had realised this herself long ago whilst sitting for long hours alone.

"I did not want to point this out to you. I am so sorry. We will talk about this further when we see each other. Papa has given me the details of when you sail and the Captain will put you down in a quiet seaside port. He will not say where in case someone talks on the way to Liverpool. He cannot risk the customs men coming aboard and finding you if he takes you all the way. When you are on English soil, is there someone you know who could help you?"

Kate had already planned this part of her journey. Her parents could not know that she was in England, or indeed alive and safe, however much it pained her to cause so much anguish to them. Her only hope was to contact her aunt, her mother's older sister, who lived alone in a small village in Cumbria. She would have to convince her to let her stay without her parents knowing her whereabouts, which would be hard for her aunt to do. *God what a mess*, she thought, not for the first time.

She answered Davido, telling him that she had an idea and would tell him when they met up. The less they talked about plans the better, as they had a habit of going wrong and only added to their worries.

He agreed and promised to keep her and his family informed of what was happening in Milan.

Kate handed the phone back to Alfredo.

All they had to do now was wait.

32

ANTONIO arrived to take Kate and Luca down to the port where it had been arranged that Davido would meet them at the trawler, which was more like a smaller version of a container ship. No one but the crew would be around and, probably, a few sailors who would be entertaining *women of the port* who would hopefully just assume Kate was one of them.

Luca was well wrapped up in a blanket and if he remained asleep would be unlikely to be noticed. Valentina, taking no chances, had given him a mild sedative. Kate had not been happy with this but knew no other way to ensure that Luca did not make a scene when she had to hand him over to Davido and walk away for ever. Valentina assured her that the sedative was often used for flying on planes by children and would not harm him in any way, so Kate had reluctantly agreed to it.

Kate's nerves were threatening to overwhelm her, as the moment had come where she would either return to her family or be caught. She had said goodbye to the Romanos who had, once again, apologised for what Davido had put her through and asked her to pray that God would forgive him and that he would not be charged with the kidnap as he had tried to make amends. She said that, although she could not forgive his part in the kidnap, he was not responsible for what happened afterwards and she was grateful to him and his family for helping her escape.

They waited in the warmth of a little hut that provided hot drinks and snacks for the dockers at all hours. No one else was there and the time seemed to go by insufferably slowly. They waited and waited and still Davido did not come. Finally the Captain arrived and asked how long it would be as they needed to get Kate aboard and settled into her cabin to set sail. They needed to go out on the tide.

They waited some more but Davido still did not come. Two hours after they had arrived at the docks the Captain returned, this time accompanied by Fredo and Valentina. Kate could see by their faces that something had gone wrong.

Fredo spoke rapidly to Antonio whilst Valentina turned to Kate. "I am sorry Anna, Davido cannot come. He is being watched by the

33
Police Headquarters, Milan, 2008

ISPETTORE Rappelli was acting like a raging bull in the squad room. His staff sat quietly waiting for the tirade to subside. Vital evidence had been lost and he wasn't happy. Sergeant Verdi was on the receiving end of it, unfairly it had to be said, having tried to explain how it might have been lost in the nineteen-seventies when protocol, possibly, hadn't been quite so strictly adhered to and cold cases not such a priority, before the use of DNA and new forensics.

Rappelli was having none of it; that was why evidence should always be meticulously catalogued at all times and preserved for all time, because of the possibility of new science in the future, that stored evidence might solve a crime. He would sack anyone that made the same mistake now, he assured them all. Valuable time would be wasted trying to recover the lost information because of someone's incompetence.

Verdi had brought up the list of signatures from Records and Rappelli assigned two officers to chasing up the names on it and finding out if any of the retired officers, who took the statements were still alive. After a short while, they came back with the information that only one of the officers was still living, who had been present at the 1978 interrogations and he had retired years ago. Usefully, however, he was notorious for keeping his own copies of notes on unsolved crimes, to peruse at his leisure.

Rappelli assigned Verdi to the task of setting up a visit to the former senior detective, a man called Vittorio Pucci, as soon as possible and getting a statement from him. Old detectives like Pucci rarely lost their thirst for solving cases and Rappelli was confident that Pucci would have kept all of his notes from his long career in the Force. He dismissed his staff with a final rant at his officers, saying how foolish the Italian police would look to their English colleagues, then slammed his door shut. He rang his son, Enzo, to vent his annoyance once again and then he rang Jasmine.

The Brite Agency was a hive of activity as Jasmine was catching up on her staff's progress with their other cases. After speaking with Ispettore Rappelli, she relayed the conversation and the information that there had been a setback in Milan, meaning they needed to get cracking on Kate's family's recollections again and assume, for the time being, that the missing statement would not crack the crime.

Jasmine asked Evie to contact June Marshall again to request another meeting. They both thought the woman was withholding something of significance, just by her demeanour, and it needed to be winkled out.

Next Jasmine set about compiling a new plan of action. *Where to go from here is the problem* she admitted to herself. *Could two people just disappear without a trace?* The sad fact was that yes, working as a Missing Persons Agent, she knew that thousands of people went missing everyday somewhere in the world, but you only got to hear about the ones who eventually turned up dead or alive. Unfortunately, Kate and Luca were obviously going to be in the former category and without a new lead, the case was going to be much harder than even she had thought. *No bodies, no evidence.* Even so, Jasmine could not shake off the feeling that Kate's parents would have continued to search and hope for ever. In other cases that she had dealt with, she had seen that the closest relatives never gave up that hope that their loved one would one day walk through their door, never moving home or getting on with their own lives, just in case. And yet June Marshall had given up it seemed. She needed to be questioned again to see why that was. How involved had the family been with the Buscolli search after the notoriety had died down?

Jasmine knew that she had never gotten over the death of her parents in an accident, an accident that, even now, was still a mystery to Hugo and herself. Why had they been where they were at the scene of the fatal car crash? Jasmine still had those unanswered questions but at least they had buried their parents and had known that they had died. The Marshalls and the Buscollis, like so many others, had not been able to do that, so how long would she have searched if she hadn't known what had happened to her own parents? She knew the answer to that question, *forever.*

She decided that this time she would interview June Marshall herself to satisfy her own curiosity.

Evie was persuasive. Although extremely reluctant, Mrs. Marshall agreed to meet again but said it would have to be the following week as she was busy. Evie agreed that would be fine, not wanting to give her the chance to refuse a meeting. Meanwhile the Brite Agency would get on with solving the whereabouts of other clients' missing relatives.

Without something from Kate's mother, Jasmine was relying on Ispettore Rappelli if the case was to progress any further. If not, it would, unfortunately, have to remain unsolved and she would have to give Santa that news soon. Although it had been always a very slim chance that they would uncover any new information, she still felt she was letting Santa down. It was always a mistake to get too personally involved with a client and their case but it was too late for that. She desperately cared about Kate and Luca now and needed to know for herself what had happened in 1978. She would ensure that she had explored every avenue possible before she gave up.

The big question now was why had a piece of valuable evidence gone missing from the case file?

Human error or something more sinister?

34

PUCCI was more than happy to be involved again with his unsolved nemesis, the Buscolli Case. He had, indeed, taken the file out just before he retired, one last time, and made notes for himself to ponder over now he had all the time in the world. He had also taken photocopies of all that the file contained, although officially that was not allowed. His retirement had, however, been fully occupied and it was only now, his wife having died a few years ago, that he had time on his hands to sit and reminisce about his time in the force.

He led Sergeant Verdi to his study where a shelf of boxed files had pride of place alongside a state of the art computer and office equipment that would put police headquarters to shame and all set out immaculately. It seemed the old detective could not let go of his status after retirement, still needing the façade of being a useful policeman in thought if not in deed. Verdi wondered how many other retirees need this comforting reassurance. Actually, these old sticklers for retaining their prior lives were becoming more and more valuable in the cold case department; nothing like the memory of a good detective to help solve an old case now forensic science had caught up.

Pucci went straight to a heavy folder, obviously filed under B, and took it from the shelf.

"Here you are. I would have photocopied all evidence for my personal perusal. Of course I knew we were not allowed but I am a person who likes to study things in my own time. I always found I did not work so well under pressure to get results quickly. Best to look at evidence after a good meal and a glass or two of excellent wine after a hard day's work."

"Thank you. We are looking for a missing statement, as I said on the telephone."

"If it was in there in 1978, then a copy of it will be here now. I'll leave you to it whilst I make coffee for us. You will find everything in perfect order so it should be easy to find what you are looking for."

It was.

Verdi picked out the typed pages that were clipped together, entitled *Romano, Davido Alfredo: Interviewed May 25th – June 3rd 1978.*

Romano had evidently been called into police headquarters several times. His movements in the summer of 1978 were all there in the statement and there was no way that it wouldn't be pored over, once again, this time to see why the originals had disappeared. Indeed, that was why Verdi needed to destroy it but there was no way to do so or even to alter it. Rappelli would be on it like a dog with a bone.

After thanking Pucci for his help and returning the file to him saying, that the statement hadn't yielded any relevant information after all, then listening to Pucci reminisce about the good old days over coffee, Verdi left to consider how to stop the boss gaining the lead in the Buscolli case. He was essentially reduced to praying that his boss would not realise what he was seeing in front of him.

Verdi drove off a short distance and stopped the car to go over the statement for a second time.

This time, there would be no way of destroying it.

The whole office was awaiting its arrival at the station.

35

TRANSCRIPT OF STATEMENT COMPILED UNDER CAUTION AT POLIZIA DI STATO, MILANO. 3rd JUNE 1978. FROM WITNESS ROMANO, DAVIDO ALFREDO. DATE OF BIRTH: - 04/04/1956. IN THE PRESENCE OF DETECTIVE VITTORIO PUCCI AND DETECTIVE BENITO NERO.

I am Davido Alfredo Romano, residing at 135 Via St. Antonio di Napoli and a student of Universita Catholica del Sacro Cuore, studying Economics and Political sciences and in my second year of study. Formerly residing in my parental home in Genova.

I have been interviewed several times concerning my friendship with Raphael Grecco. I state that my friendship with him began when we both started university together and has continued until these terrible circumstances. We both attended political science lectures together and became firm friends but from the early days I recognised his fervour for current Italian political unrest and a particular interest in Brigade Rosse and other subversive organisations and I distanced myself away from his fervour merely disagreeing, mildly, with his views over our birre. I saw them as dangerous and ill-informed and told him so.

Gradually as he got more involved with a group of older people that hung around the bars near the campus I saw less of him and more of my girlfriend alone. I admit to having been seen on occasion with these people but it was not to my liking and only to keep Raphael company.

I state, on record, that I have no interest in Brigate Rosse or any similar faction, and am deeply ashamed to have been the friend of someone who could carry out such a heinous crime, for which, I have now been implicated as guilty by association.

I further state that on the 9th May of this year, I was in university in my lecture, verifiable by my fellow students and tutor. I was there all day and left at 5.30 p.m. to meet my girlfriend who works at Ferrellis department store. Then we went for a meal at Taverna Toscani in the centre of Milano until I walked her home and returned to my room at 9 p.m. The caretaker has verified that this is so.

The next morning and every day since I have attended university and remained in the city and available for police interviews. I learnt of Raphael's involvement with the Buscolli kidnapping and his death the morning it was in the newspaper and the university was alive with the news.

I was extremely shocked having met Kate Marshall and the child some months earlier when Raphael met her for the first time outside Il Duomo, on the steps. She was with another girl but I do not remember her name as I had no interest in her as I have a girlfriend.

I did not see them again but knew Raphael was meeting up with Kate. I assumed that he liked her but was not serious about her as she was a foreign girl and nothing could come of it. When we had first met the two girls he had made a comment that English girls were good for fun but not for marriage; they gave themselves freely to any boy. He did not respect them and those are his thoughts, not mine.

I profess, in this statement witnessed and in the company of Detectives' Pucci and Nero and in the presence of Almighty God, whom I am answerable too, that I am innocent of any involvement in the kidnapping of Luca Buscolli and Kate Marshall.

Signed: *D.A.Romano*

At the foot of the statement, Pucci had added a postscript stating that after intense interrogation over several days, Davido Romano was considered innocent of any involvement and having no knowledge of the crime, could be of no further help, and so was free to carry on with his own life, without his name being brought into the public domain. No further action was needed and he was free to go.

that way. It might be a wild goose chase, but it might not. He felt in his guts that they were on to something at last.

Verdi made a phone call that evening. "It's started; say nothing. The police are on their way."

Fredo Romano slowly replaced the handset and sat shakily, down at the table, calling out to his wife.

37

JASMINE arrived with Evie just after 10.30 a.m. as they had had to drop Evie's daughter off at school before setting off to June Marshall's, neat but soulless home.

The door was opened by an older woman who introduced herself as Maggie Tunstall, June's elder sister, who ushered them into the sitting room where her sister sat wringing her hands, nervously. The sisters were as different as chalk and cheese. With about a ten a year difference in age, Maggie was short, plump and had the ruddy complexion of someone who had spent most of their life outdoors. June, in contrast, looked as though she didn't let much sunlight into hers.

Maggie immediately took charge of the conversation. "Misses. Brite and Baxter, I must first say that I think this is a great intrusion into my sister's life. You have brought back all the pain and distress of thirty years ago. I hope you are proud of yourselves."

She remained standing, arms folded.

"I apologise to you both for our return visit and I promise we will bother you no further, but there has been an unexpected development in our information, that was not pursued in 1978 and might have been of relevance. It may lead to progress in our finding out what happened after your daughter's kidnapping. We are anxious to see if you think it at all plausible to pursue this line of enquiry."

"And what would that be?" June asked, sceptically or warily. Jasmine couldn't decide which it was. Something was definitely not right about her reaction to the news.

"Well, the Italian policeman that is helping us with our case, has unearthed a missing statement from the time of the crime that had been removed from the files or simply got lost over the years. We are pursuing the idea that if it was taken out deliberately by someone in police force, then it contained vital information that had been missed. Of course, we may be wrong but it is worth looking into any clue, however small," Jasmine said.

"What is this clue?" asked Maggie, still with her arms folded but at least she was now sitting down and seemingly willing to listen.

"The statement contained the information that a witness's home town was Genoa, not too far from Milan. It's a large fishing and cargo port. Now, the Italian Inspector on the case and I think it is worth going to Genoa to seek out the man's family home and see if he returned there. He seems to have vanished after 1978. The Milanese police can find no address or social security number, employment record or any trace of him, which in itself is odd. Of course, following his original interviews the police officers had no reason to doubt his innocence and I am not saying he is not innocent but we would like to speak to him.

"What I am about to suggest may offend you, and for that I can only apologise, but in order to do the best I can for Santa Buscolli I must explore every possibility, however extreme."

"Go on, Miss Brite, do your worst" Maggie said, coldly.

"We must go back to the Milan of 1978 to understand what might have happened. As you witnessed yourself, June, the Italian papers were having a media frenzy about the case. They were implying that Kate was part of the gang responsible for the kidnapping. After all, she had the perfect opportunity. She had been told not to see Raphael Grecco but continued to do so despite being at risk of losing her job. The media also compared your daughter's kidnapping to that of the American heiress, Patty Hearst, in 1974 who was captured by the Symbionese Liberation Army and spent nineteen months with her captors, joining them in criminal acts soon. She had effectively become sympathetic to their cause. The press suggested that Kate could also have been influenced by Grecco and his friends and coerced into kidnapping the boy, on the understanding that he would be returned immediately and no harm would come to him."

"Preposterous! How dare you!" June shouted.

"Please, Mrs. Marshall. I am only saying what you know already and saw yourself."

"My daughter would never ever contemplate such a thing. She was a good decent girl who was young and naïve, in a foreign country all on her own. She was treated as a criminal not a victim and here you are doing the same again! Enough, I want you out of my house."

June stood up but her sister gently pulled her down again. "Please, we must hear her out, however awful and unjust her theory is. Then we can be rid of the Brite Agency for good and get on with our lives once more."

June subsided, allowing her sister to put her arm around her and Jasmine continued.

"Think back, Mrs. Marshal. Did Kate ever mention in her letters the almost weekly attacks in Milan by the Red Brigade and its supporters; Brigate Rosse, she would have called them. Did she comment on the state of Italian politics and the dissatisfaction of the young Milanese she was mixing with, anything at all that might have suggested the kind of person Grecco was?"

"She would not have written about any of that to me and I cannot believe she would have been interested. She was eighteen, for God's sake. Interested in boys and the fact that she was in one of the fashion capitals of the world and oblivious to politics and any corruption. She did say that all Italians seemed to be genuinely scared of the Mafia and it was not like *The Godfather* film with dashing Al Pacino lookalikes, but that was in jest and a throw away comment. She wrote that she was happy and in love with Raphael and that was what we, her father and I, were most worried about in case she decided to marry him and stay in Milan, or God forbid, get pregnant. That was what concerned us in her letters. We missed her terribly."

"I do not wish to hurt or distress you with this conversation but I have to continue with this line of enquiry all the same. Think about it. Do our parents ever know the person we present to our friends? Your daughter had effectively grown up and was responsible for all her actions and she was totally without family to guide her. An Italian lifestyle was very far removed from what she was used to at home. She had to learn a new language to be understood by most Italians except her employers. She would be used to being wary of the police who were not regarded as *the friendly copper in the street* as they were by most English people, unless you were a criminal. The Milanese policemen carried visible guns and were licenced to use them. An unpaid metro fare or tram fare could land you at the police station convicted of theft not a telling off by the conductor. She would have been told how different things were in Milan by her employers and Raphael. You must look at it from a different perspective. She may easily have been influenced by the young, intelligent students she was meeting and I'm sorry to point out again, you could not know the grown-up she had become over there."

"My daughter would not do such a thing for such a mercenary reason as money for terrorists. I do know that for certain, Miss Brite."

Jasmine continued, "I understand your feelings and am sorry. We will not trouble you again, Mrs Marshall and I apologise for the distress it's caused."

Jasmine and Evie stood up, offering to shake the hand of June Marshall but she declined and Maggie Tunstall led them out to the front door. Without a further word she slammed it shut behind them.

Back in the car, Evie observed, "June didn't ask where your questioning was going. Wonder why?"

Jasmine and Evie had discussed putting the theory that Kate and Davido Romano had actually been part of the kidnapping of Luca Buscolli and finding out that the rest of the gang were dead, had decided to flee to Genoa. Jasmine said, "I decided, the way things were going, not to suggest our theory to Mrs. Marshal, but it remains a possibility, nonetheless, that hopefully Vincenzo Rappelli will investigate in Genoa. What I'm sure about is that June Marshall and her sister are hiding something."

Of that she was positive.

38

IT was an early start for the two Rappellis as they were anxious to get to Genoa in time for the local dock workers breakfast break, the time that they would be most likely to catch the Romano family at home but not as intrusive as turning up during the family main meal. Co-operation was key as their questioning would, once again, imply that Davido Romano was a suspect.

Jasmine had called earlier after her meeting with June Marshall, as they were on their way to Genoa, and told him of her suspicions. He had agreed that the sisters' reaction seemed odd. Although having every right to feel affronted, their unwillingness to help the investigation at all was unexpected. It was if they had decided that Kate's fate would never be known and that they had moved on. It was a strange assumption for a mother to have. In the experience of both the agency and the police, parents of missing children usually died before giving up the hope that they would one day be re-united with them; that they would be found. There was a small chance that finding Davido Romano might lead somewhere, so surely Kate's family ought to be praying that it would and be willing to help the investigation. It seemed not.

It was a little after 11.30 a.m., later than they would have liked. The traffic had been horrendous. Everyone seemed to be heading for the coast and away from the unbearable city heat. The men they wanted to speak to might have already returned to work until the afternoon siesta break, at the hottest part of the day but he Rappellis would chance it anyway.

Vincenzo had obtained the address of the Romano family home. It had been passed down to the eldest son after Alfredo Romano had died in 1996. He had been the father of seven sons, a fact he had apparently whole-heartedly embraced and boasted about with pride, continuing the Romano name which could be traced back to the earliest of Genoese history.

The Rappellis took a leisurely stroll, having had to leave the car at the port car park. They asked a local shopkeeper the whereabouts of the Romano house in the maze of narrow streets and alleys but still nearly missed the door hidden unobtrusively flush with the ancient alley wall.

They knocked on it loudly with confidence.

It was opened after half a minute by a woman, probably in her late fifties, but who had the look of early aging brought on by a hard life, as many Italian working-class women did.

"Prego?" she asked.

"Buon Giorno, Signora. Scusarci per l'intrusione non annuciata," Vincenzo said, apologetically. He proceeded to introduce himself and his son as officers from Milan who were in the process at looking again at the Buscolli case of 1978, having received new evidence.

This was not strictly true but he thought that if the Romanos did have anything to hide this would worry them.

Valentina Romano introduced herself as Fredo Romano's wife and ushered them in. A man of about sixty, or looking it, sat at the kitchen table reading a newspaper. He indicated that they should sit down and Valentina offered them coffee. They thanked her and explained again to Fredo Romano why they were there, asking him first who still lived at the house, as they were anxious to speak to all the brothers if possible.

"Only Valentina and I live here, Ispettore . My five brothers live near the port with their families."

"Five brothers? It is my understanding that you have six."

"Did have, Ispettore. Davido sadly drowned many years ago."

Valentina came to sit at the table where she placed a pot of fresh coffee and two more cups. "You have his death on your conscience, I hope," she added, bitterly.

"How so, signora?" asked Vincenzo, surprised at both the accusation and the knowledge that Davido Romano was dead.

"The Buscolli case weighed heavily on him. His friend was not who he thought him to be, so he found it difficult to continue his studies with the suspicion by his fellow students that there was no smoke without fire, hanging over him. He returned here but he could not settle where his hopes of a better life had led him back to poverty and, of course, your police had been brutal and he was not a boy who dealt with violence easily. His experiences in the army had made him a pacifist. He was a gentle, innocent, academic boy," she explained, angrily.

Enzo Rappelli had not entered the conversation, so far, but he felt the need to support his father in the unfair accusation that he had been in any way involved in the treatment of Davido Romano in

1978. He felt indignant for his father's sake. "We are sorry for your loss, Signora Romano, but my father was not involved in any way with the interrogation of the suspects. Your brother-in-law was one of them, and not to excuse harsh treatment, the Buscolli case was very sensitive; people were dead and a child and his English teenage nanny were missing, possibly dead also. Any information gained could have found them alive and time was of the essence, don't you agree? Sometimes force is the only way to decide whether a suspect is guilty or innocent. Well it was in 1978. We do not procure statements in this way nowadays, of course. Times were very different then I am sorry to say."

The Romanos stayed silent.

"I am sorry to distress you both, especially after hearing that the person we were hoping to speak to is no longer alive." Vincenzo took over the questioning from his son. "I must explain that we have recently uncovered a statement from Davido that appears to have been taken or lost from our files, we cannot say which, but it is extremely unusual to mislay documents, as they are signed in and out every time an officer handles the files, so that evidence is not lost or damaged, precisely because with new detection techniques such as DNA sampling, old cases can now be re-examined. We are acting on the premise that the statement was taken for a reason by an officer and we needed to speak to Davido to see if he knew why this might have happened. Did he know an officer that might have thought he was somehow helping him by removing his name from the investigation? Possibly with good intentions for Davido's future career, as he would not want a record of his association with the kidnapping, however slight, to come to light if he was innocent, as you say."

This explanation seemed to pacify the couple. They nodded their heads in unison. "That could have happened, I suppose, as you point out," Fredo said. "Davido's name on police records could have damaged his reputation and prevented him achieving his goals. Perhaps that is what he most feared and why he did not continue his studies. My poor brother had so much to be proud of and the Buscollis and your police took it away from him, all because of his friend's crimes. He came back a broken man. I do not see how we can help you, Ispettore Rappelli, so I would like it if you would leave my home now"

Fredo got up from the table, with a dismissive gesture. The two policemen stood following his lead and Signora Romano ushered them back to the front door.

Outside in the alley, Enzo looked at his father in despair. "What now, Papa?" he asked.

"We go down into Low town, son, and see what we can find out about this drowning."

They threaded their way as quickly as they could through the narrow streets and the melee of tourists towards the portside cafés and bars in search of one that looked most likely to be frequented by locals. It wasn't hard to spot. As Vincenzo and Enzo walked into the bar, all conversation stopped. As usual, their status as police officers was apparent to the clientele. It never failed to astonish the two men, and most of their colleagues, just how much they stood out. Was it their walk? Their demeanour? Who knew but it was like a scent of the elite authoritarian, mistrusted and disliked by almost every civilian in Italy and could not be disguised?

They approached the barman and asked for two beers. He placed them silently on the bar together with a bowl of peanuts and another with olives.

"Don't worry lads," Vincenzo addressed the whole bar. "My son and I are on holiday here; not in any official capacity, so relax."

It took several seconds but the conversations around him resumed. Even policemen were entitled to a holiday, it seemed.

They picked up their drinks and sat at a table just outside, each contemplating how they would get any information from the hostile dockers, if this was not to be a totally wasted journey.

Enzo suggested, "Papa, I think we are in the wrong bar. Perhaps a stroll along the dockside might be more profitable?"

"Perhaps, son, but give it time. I won't give up yet. I want to find out more about the Romano brothers, I suspect their old family status commands a certain amount of respect and maybe envy in this area? Perhaps someone might be willing to talk about Davido's demise. It must have been a tragedy here, his being so young and a Romano, even when they are so used to deaths at sea."

They finished their beers and went back inside. This time, no one reacted.

Vincenzo ordered another beer and a coffee for Enzo who would be driving them back to Milan and a plate of pre-packed prosciutto con salade in a panini, the only food seemly on sale behind the bar. This was fair enough as anyone desiring a more filling meal could frequent any one of the other restaurants or tourist cafes lining the port's promenade.

They sat at a table inside this time and listened to the conversations going on around them. After a while one of the older men asked them if they often visited Genoa, as it was close to Milan and he had noticed their distinct Milanese accents.

Vincenzo said, "Yes, I often travelled here with my family to escape the summer heat of the city, when my sons were young. It is such a beautiful part of the Italian Riviera," he added, "full of history and ancient family heritage. Milan, in contrast, is truly cosmopolitan and perhaps because of this, has lost some of its charisma and appeal, which is a pity as it has much to offer, if you are prepared to look for it."

The man agreed wholeheartedly and said most of the fishermen and dockers were carrying on a family tradition that spanned centuries, since the first Genoese civilization, the sea always providing sustenance and a living for its residents.

Vincenzo and Enzo continued the conversation in this vein until Enzo decided it was worth mentioning the Romano family, saying he had known a nephew of theirs who lived in Milan.

"Ah, yes, the Romano family are a force to be reckoned with. Seven sons, Alfredo had. All dockers and their sons too. They are all well known here, usually coming in after work. They can get a bit rowdy when they've been drinking, very loyal to each other, so it sometimes ends in a fight, but that is family, no? They have not been without tragedy though. One son drowned years ago and that hit them hard and, of course, when old Alfredo died his funeral was attended by so many people that the church could not hold them. A loudspeaker was used for the people outside to hear the service. The poor man deteriorated after his son died. He never really got over it." He shook his head in sadness.

"Did many people come to his son's funeral too?" Enzo asked, interrupting the man's reminiscence.

"No, his body was never recovered from the sea. He went out one night on a trawler and fell overboard, or so it was thought, but rumours went around that he had committed suicide. Of course, no one said that within the Romanos hearing - a dreadful sin to do that in the eyes of God. He would not have gone to heaven. The Romanos are God fearing Catholics, as are most of us Genoese."

"So sad to lose a child," Vincenzo reflected. "I do not think I could stand the loss of one of my sons, either. Poor Alfredo Romano."

"Yes, tragic indeed. Oh well, we have truly entered dark waters. I apologise. I merely wanted to engage you in conversation. It does not do our Genoese hospitality good to ignore our tourists, but you have stepped into a rather domestic drinking hole. Better to dine further along or more happily in High town, in its beautiful surroundings."

"We will take your advice, thank you" Vincenzo said. Then they both finished off their meal and drinks and discussed more general topics before getting up, shaking the stranger's hand and stepping out once more into the blistering heat of the day.

39

THE two men made their way towards the portside which was a hive of activity, with cruise ships discharging their passengers via smaller crafts and fishermen busy attending to their boats, after the morning catch had been removed and packed in ice ready for transport. The whole area stank of its main trade and Enzo's nose protested. His delicate palette was unaccustomed to the smell of a hard living; he preferred his fish swimming in lemon juice and herbs. Vincenzo smiled at his son's obvious distaste and punched him lightly on the shoulder. "You have been spoiled and protected from the realities of your dinner plate, my boy. Lucky for you, we are a family of police officers, eh?"

"Yes Papa, I have only the smell of death and the autopsy room to look forward to. How delicate, I am," he replied, sarcastically, annoyed at his father's chiding.

They stood watching for a while lost in their own thoughts until, eventually, someone hosing down the nearest fishing boat asked them if they were looking for someone and could he help?

Vincenzo asked where the shipping office could be found? He had decided that the way forward, if they were to take a look at the shipping logs that recorded incoming and outgoing craft and their cargo for 1978, was to ask politely, as it was an unofficial request. It was a place to start and he could think of nothing else that might help.

The fisherman pointed further down the docks to a building reached by a set of steps, so that the windows overlooked the port and its goings on. They knocked on the door and entered when a booming and impatient voice shouted, "Avanti!."

"Scusi, Signore, I have a request if you could spare a moment of your time?" Vincenzo asked, politely.

"I have little time, Signore. What is it you want and who are you?" replied the man in front of them. He was dressed officially in Naval uniform, implying he was a man of importance, Enzo thought wryly, if a little unfairly. He would have felt more at home in his own uniform as the officer had so far totally ignored him and it stung, especially after his father's remark earlier.

"I am Ispettore Rappelli of the Polizia di Stato, Milano and this is my fellow officer and son, Enzo Rappelli. We are here in Genoa in an unofficial capacity, investigating an old case that has recently been re-opened by a Missing Persons Agency in England. You are under no obligation to help but it would be appreciated if we could take a look at your log books for 1978, as this is the year we are interested in. I must admit that we are at somewhat of a standstill with the case again and searching your logs is our final action before admitting defeat."

"Well you can see I am a very busy man. I have no time for such things Why were they not looked at in 1978?"

"Sadly, an error at the time meant Genoa was not a location that was considered relevant. Information has now come to light thirty years later. It may be nothing but we would like to explore every avenue, you understand?"

"What is this case?"

"Alas Signore, I cannot reveal that. It is sensitive."

The Port Master looked at them, silently deciding whether he wished to help, not knowing the case in question and not being able to satisfy his own curiosity, now it had been aroused. Finally, he huffed dismissively and said he would get his assistant to search for the required log books if they were prepared to come back after lunch.

They agreed to return at 4 p.m. after the afternoon siesta, so he bid them good day and the Rappellis left, satisfied that they would be able to search for what they were looking for, even if they had to wait.

They decided to explore High Town and indulge in a meal at a good restaurant to pass the time.

At 4 p.m. on the dot they were back at the Port Master's office.

He was not there but a young man was sitting at his desk.

"Ah, you must be the police officers. Port Master Giraldo informed me that you would be coming for a look at our log books for 1978. I have spent my lunch hour digging them out for you. As you probably gather, all our records since the nineties have gradually been transferred to our computer files at central office but we have not reached as far back as the seventies yet but we run a very tight ship here and the correct log books were easily found in the store rooms, although they were a little dusty," the clerk said with a smile.

"Thank you, Signore, I am most grateful for your diligence," replied Vincenzo. "Would it be easier if we took them away with us and return them in due course?"

"No, no, Ispettore. Signore Giraldo has left instructions that they must remain in my sight. After all, we have only your word that you are here unofficially for what we do not know, and he did comment that you had lost certain important documents before. I'm sorry but I must insist you stay here. It is a discretionary favour we are allowing. These are private and official records. May I see your identification before I hand them over please and then you can sit at my desk in the corner and read them at your leisure, though of course we close in a few hours."

Vincenzo, anxious to cooperate, smiled and said, of course and that he was pleased the clerk was being so professionally cautious. Their identification confirmed, via their police badges and identity cards, they squeezed themselves around the little desk and began to study the massive logbooks, not really knowing what they were looking for but hoping something would stand out.

As they got to May 1978 they slowed down and examined each entry in detail. They were becoming familiar with the names of craft and captains that were regularly in and out of the port. They were particularly interested in smaller boats and trawlers that could go about their business with comparative ease, as there were less security measures back in the seventies to adhere to, before mass illegal immigration had become a problem and searches were not a priority for familiar craft. These were Genoese fishermen and cargo boats that made their living, just as their ancestors had, beyond suspicion by their fellow Genoese officers, who were easily persuaded to turn a blind eye to a little contraband for the right price.

One particular name stood out for Enzo for the time they were interested in. This was a small cargo ship owned by Teti & Sons, which travelled regularly to Liverpool, England docking there to deliver goods, waiting a few days to load industrial cargo from Liverpool and then head back to Genoa where the whole process would begin again. It was regular transportation, so the Teti company clearly had a good business reputation and was probably one of the older family firms in Genoa. It transported a variety of goods and general produce and was probably a cheaper way for smaller businesses to import and export rather than using the big companies. Genoa was and, still was in 2008, the main seaport on the Mediterranean Sea. In 1978 it would not have been as colossal and important as now but it would still have been vibrant and industrious.

40

2nd June, 1978

THE night sky was surprisingly bright, filled with stars and no cloud, beautiful, in fact, but lost on Kate. The captain had tried in vain to get some information from her, but had finally given up when Kate professed not to understand anything he was saying, apart from the very basic English that he probably used in business transactions. After making her and Luca as comfortable as possible in his cabin he left her to it. Luca was soon settled again, having, it seemed, gotten used to his strange and varied living arrangements. Soon Kate fell asleep herself, from sheer exhaustion and worry.

Luca awoke as daylight seeped through the tiny porthole. Kate had slept sporadically, her mind unwilling to switch off and her dreams full of horror. She washed up and saw to Luca's needs in the small bathroom, little more than a cupboard but obviously the captain's privilege.

A knock on door announced the captain. He entered with a mug of coffee, milk for Luca and two pastries. Kate thanked him and asked where they were, via basic Italian and hand gestures.

"Wales, signora. You will be arriving soon."

"Arriving where?" asked an alarmed Kate.

The captain looked perplexed then said, "Prego, signora. I get Luigi, he speak the English better." He left her to go and fetch Luigi.

Soon, a young man entered the cabin. "Buon giorno, signora. The captain has asked me to explain that we cannot take you into Liverpool docks. We will be boarded by customs and excise officers looking for contraband, you understand? You will be put ashore near Bangor, a small seaport where we have anchored before without trouble."

Kate sat silently ingesting this information. It would make little difference to her plans where she was put ashore, as she would be contacting her aunt Maggie and asking for her help. As long as she was on British soil she would feel safer. She thanked Luigi and asked if he could explain to the captain that she had only Italian lira on her and did he have any sterling that she could exchange it for, as she needed to make arrangements to travel once she was ashore. He replied that he would tell the captain, wished her good luck and left.

So, it was, that a little over an hour later, Kate and Luca were lowered in to a small wooden lifeboat by a boatman who rowed them towards a secluded bay. It was still early, just after 6 a.m., and the shore was deserted, but for a solitary figure approaching the incoming boat. The boatman helped Kate and Luca ashore. Then the two men spoke and money was exchanged. *This is clearly a common occurrence*, thought Kate. *Perhaps a bit of regular smuggling goes on here.*

The stranger did not look like a seaman; more of a lifeguard, young and muscular. He didn't speak, but led Kate, with Luca in her arms, up the beach and to a hut that was probably the lifeguard lookout post. He opened the door and told her to sit down as he put the kettle on and made them some tea. He said, "I don't want to know anything at all about you. I don't get involved with the Teti's business. It's better that way." He told her to sit and drink her tea and then she should make her way up the steps to the road above the beach.

After that he left.

Kate sat awhile comforting a confused Luca and gathering her thoughts together. The captain had been generous with the exchange of her money, so she decided to go into the town and find a telephone kiosk so she call her aunt and then get themselves some breakfast at a café.

She wished that she had a pushchair for Luca as it was tiring and laborious carrying him for most of the time. It was a lot to ask of his little legs to walk so far, but it was unavoidable. Fortunately, he was taking everything in his stride and was eager to leave the hut and explore his sandy surroundings. There were steps up from the hut that led to a little lane that came out by a tourist shop, selling buckets and spades, rubber rings, flags and all the other paraphernalia holidaymakers might desire. Kate didn't go in but continued along the lane.

As they re-joined civilization, she spotted a public telephone box that was close to a crazy golf course, that Luca got excited about. She went into the kiosk, sat Luca on the shelf beside the telephone and picked up the receiver to dial the operator. She asked for help locating a phone number for her aunt's farm in Cumbria. She gave the address and was given the number within seconds. Then Kate requested a reverse call to her aunt, saying it was her niece on the line.

The operator told her to wait on the line whilst she asked the telephone owner if she would accept the call. A minute later, she heard her aunt's voice and felt like crying with relief but, for Luca's sake, she kept it together.

"Aunt Maggie, please don't say anything. I will explain when I, hopefully, see you. I am in a little town near Bangor, Wales. I need your help; please can you come and fetch me. Do not tell anyone where I am. Not even my parents. Please I beg of you."

Silence met her on the phone. *Have I made a terrible mistake?* She thought, in a panic.

"My dear child, thank God!" her aunt, finally, exclaimed and let out an enormous sob.

"Please don't say anything but that you will come. I feel so alone but glad to be here." Kate interrupted her distraught aunt.

"Yes! Yes. Where are you?"

Kate gave the name of the little town and the name of the café near the telephone kiosk. "Thank you, Aunt Maggie, I love you." With that she put the phone down, unable to carry on speaking.

She took a moment to pull herself together, then lifted Luca down from the shelf and kissed him. "Come on, Luca let's go and eat and then we can come and play crazy golf, won't that be fun?"

They sat and had breakfast in the nearby café and waited until the crazy golf opened for the day. It was heart-warming to hear Luca squeal with delight as they played in the sunshine. A simple joy but so welcome after the chaos of the last few weeks. It gave her hope that he would forget their ordeal, if he even realised that there had been one.

She would not be so lucky.

41

LATE afternoon, as the sun was going down on what had been a hot day spent on the beach, splashing in the sea and making sandcastles, they made their way, once again, to the little café that Kate's Aunt Maggie had arranged to meet them in. The journey from Cumbria would have only taken about three hours but, of course, Kate's aunt would have had to organise the necessary help around her farm whilst she was away. Her aunt kept a few livestock that would need feeding but Kate didn't know much more, as her aunt was a bit of a recluse and the farm was remote, ideal for what Kate needed now.

As they were eating, the café's doorbell tinged an arrival and Aunt Maggie breezed in. She almost ran to her niece but stopped frozen to the spot as she saw her niece was now a very thin, short-haired brunette with a little boy sitting beside her.

Kate beckoned her over to their table. The little café was packed so she needed her aunt to make as little fuss as possible, which she did, seemingly in shock.

"Hello Aunt Maggie, thank you for coming. We'll finish up here, then take a walk, shall we?" Kate greeted her aunt, nervously.

Her aunt didn't reply but sat down, still gazing at the boy who was devouring a jam scone with relish, oblivious to the stranger who had joined them. As quickly as possible, they all left the café heading for the car Aunt Maggie had parked the car near the seafront.

Kate held Luca's hand tightly, once again, wishing that she had a pushchair with her as he was tired and getting fractious. As they reached the seafront Aunt Maggie turned towards Kate and said, "Before you tell me what's happened to you, please explain to me how you could possibly have taken this poor child away from his family and home? Whatever possessed you to do such a heinous thing?"

Kate burst into tears. Luca looked at her and attempted to comfort her as she picked him up in her arms. This little boy, who she loved so much and had so wronged by taking him with her, would he ever forgive her? Could she ever forgive herself? Utter helplessness overcame her as the enormity of her actions hit her, and as the few passers-by glanced at her with concern, her aunt ushered her into the front passenger seat of the car, placed Luca in the back seat and covered him with a blanket, cooing soothing noises to the confused child. Finally, when her silent tears subsided enough for Luca to fall asleep, satisfied that all was well again, Kate told her aunt everything.

As they talked, Luca slumbered on and Aunt Maggie remained silent as Kate explained her ordeal and her decision to keep Lucas with her. Finally, she grew silent and awaited judgement.

Aunt Maggie leaned over and embraced her niece. She was unsure of what or how to say what the poor girl needed to hear. She was deeply shocked by it all. Weeks had gone by after her sister, June, had rung to say that Kate had been kidnapped in Milan along with her charge, weeks of distraught fear on their part, expecting the worst, hoping for the best but never, ever in their wildest imaginings expecting such an outcome as this. Elation that her niece and her little charge were alive and sheer terror at the crime her niece had now committed, in escaping Milan and all the implications that now faced them. *What now?* she questioned herself.

"Are you absolutely certain that there is no way that you can return Luca to his parents without returning to Italy? No one who can help present your case?"

"I have already explained to you why I can't" replied Kate, forlornly. "The justice system isn't like ours. I would be put straight into prison as they are allowed to do that without evidence first. I have no proof at all that I wasn't involved in the kidnapping and the Italian press were baying for my blood. Marcello Buscolli is very influential and he, more or less, accused me himself. You saw the newspapers. Also, don't forget I have told you that his family has connections to the mafia in the South. That is why he had agreed to take Luca in the first place; favours aunt, favours. He is a very angry man. I would not be safe. I promise you Aunt Maggie that I love Luca with all my heart. I love him more than his so-called family and I will do everything I can to make it up to him, if you will only help us disappear."

"You are asking a hell of a lot from me, Kate. Let me think," her distressed aunt replied. They sat in silence for a long time.

"Alright, I will take you both home with me and we will devise a plan. Are you quite sure that I cannot contact your parents and at least tell them you are alive and safe?" she said, finally.

"Not yet, but I promise I will tell them as soon as I can, when I can be sure that no one is looking for us anymore. I know that I'm asking almost the impossible of you, but I can't think of another way to survive this terrible mess. I didn't want this to happen and I must live with the fact that my foolish and childish romantic crush on a complete stranger, in a strange country has led me to this unimaginable crime I must commit but I swear that I will try my very best to give Luca a wonderful life, that will be filled with love and care. I am so, so sorry for everything Aunt Maggie, I really am."

"I know child, I know." Her aunt patted her on the knee, took a deep breath and started the car that would take them towards their future, Kate, Luca and Maggie herself, whatever that held for them.

42

Polizia di Stato, Milano. 2008

AN air of excitement prevailed at the station. News had got around that Ispettore Rappelli had come in to work smiling and gathered his staff into his office to announce that the 1978 Buscolli kidnapping case had had an unexpected breakthrough and he would be working on it in collaboration with a British missing person agency. Everyone was in good cheer. It was always the way, when it seemed a cold case might at last be put to rest. It was never a good result for the station and its police force, when a high-profile case remained unsolved. They had been vastly criticised at the time by the citizens of Milan, egged on by the press, of course.

Only Sergeant Verdi was in low spirits. Fortunately, though, no one noticed. Despite having fore-warned the Romanos, it appeared that the truth had been uncovered.

Rappelli told his staff to go about their business and then he got himself a large expresso and closed the door to his office. He settled into his chair and called Jasmine.

Jasmine could not believe what she heard. A breakthrough so profound that without Vincent Rappelli and his son, Enzo's, unerring help, would never have come to light. Together they may be about to solve the case of missing Luca Buscolli and Kate Marshall, in a way she could never have imagined. Kate and Luca came to England! Not only that, but there was a distinct possibility that the two were still alive, a wonderous result, if perplexing. What on earth had happened in those intervening thirty years?

It was now up to her team to find out. She called them all to attention, which wasn't really needed as they had been listening, avidly, to her replies to the phone call she had received from the Ispettore, sensing something dramatic had happened.

Vincenzo had, during his revelation, also pointed out that having almost certainly taken Luca to England, it seemed that the press and police at the time, may have been right all along. She was, indeed, part of the gang and thus, fearing her own imprisonment, had fled taking the boy with her rather than risk being caught. It would be better to disappear altogether, along with Davido Romano and any more of the remaining gang, if there were any. As Kate was undeniably

Raphael Grecco's girlfriend and Davido Romano his friend, Jasmine had to agree the theory was entirely plausible; a faked kidnap by the most trusted of employees, the nanny.

Jasmine quickly filled in her staff as to what had been discovered in Genoa and then asked them for feedback.

"Well, the first person we should talk to about this is June Marshall, of course." said Evie. "I knew something didn't add up with her, or her sister. They were too defensive by far."

"Yes, good work Evie in spotting it straight away. We need to go carefully though and not just blunder in. We don't want either of them to know what we've found out, or should I say, may have, as we can't be sure yet that this is what happened. We need proof. When we do confront them, we need to do so unannounced." Jasmine replied. "Hugo, can you find out exactly where Maggie Tunstall lives and any information about her? We'll start with that side of the family, she seemed to get involved with our meeting with June pretty damn quickly."

"Is there anything I can do?" Caro asked.

"Not yet Caro. You man the fort here with Maddie whilst Evie and I go and pay a visit to June Marshall and try and get at the truth, if she knows it. We can't be sure of anything yet, so we must tread carefully. We don't know what happened thirty years ago or what happened to Kate and Luca but I aim to learn a lot more by the end of the day."

Jasmine could not keep the air of excitement out of her voice. This result was beyond her wildest dreams if the two were still alive. She had never hoped for that at all, just closure for poor Santa Buscolli, who, whatever the outcome of this case, would have to learn that Luca was not her brother after all.

It didn't take long for Hugo to find out that Maggie Tunstall was a seventy-four-year old spinster who had lived all her life on the family farm in an isolated part of the Cumbrian countryside. Jasmine realised that it was an achievable distance to travel and collect a young girl and a small child, from where they had been put ashore by an Italian cargo boat.

"About two and a half hours away on the motorway," Hugo interjected, as they discussed the latest development.

Perfectly feasible, thought Jasmine; *now to get the ball rolling as soon as possible.* She thanked Hugo and got back onto the phone to Vincenzo to inform him of her plans, having promised to fully co-operate with him. This would now become an official Italian police matter as well as her case.

Vincenzo advised caution as he didn't want Kate, if it was indeed Kate and Luca, to be alerted and given an opportunity to run. June and Maggie had already been made aware that the case had been reopened and would be on their guard already.

"Do you really think that Kate could have been living in England all this time?" asked Jasmine, as much to herself as to Vincenzo.

"I do not need to tell you, of all people, how easy it is to go missing and never to be heard of again. You deal with this every day. Many just get tired of the old lives and start again. Not all are victims of crime. Don't forget in all this, that Kate was still only a teenager. Her actions were not those of a mature adult. What we see now as indefensible actions might not have been seen in the same way by a child alone and frightened, and naturally, her family would have protected her, wouldn't you? I would not like to be faced with such an option in protecting one of my sons. I know, with all honesty, that I would have to think long and hard before handing one of them over to our police - sadly, as I am one of them."

"Yes, I understand you perfectly. Better to leave the passing of judgement to the professionals, if this case reaches a conclusion. What do you suggest we do now then?"

"Well, we have a little time to organise ourselves as no one but us knows we have this information. So, I suggest that you wait until myself and a fellow officer - not Enzo, although I'm sure he would jump at the chance of seeing you, but he is a traffic controller and this is now a serious investigation. I will be able to come to you in a few days, when I have organized my absence from the station, and then together we will take a look at this Maggie Tunstall's farm, agreed?"

Although she was a little deflated at having to postpone immediate action, she sighed and said, "Agreed, keep in touch and tell Enzo how sorry I am that he cannot accompany you this time."

She got off the phone and told her disappointed staff where things stood. They had also been caught up in the excitement and must now continue with more mundane, but to their clients, equally important, cases that had since come in.

43
Polizia di Stato, Milano

"RIGHT, which of you has a passport?" Vincenzo asked his assembled staff, "and is able to accompany me to England at short notice, without a wife or girlfriend protesting about your absence?"

"Me, Sir!" Verdi, almost shouted, enthusiastically. "I would be most grateful for the opportunity, Sir."

"It's not a holiday, Verdi." Vincenzo replied, sternly. "But yes, okay. I suspect most of you haven't got a passport anyway," he remarked with a sigh. It was common knowledge that many Italians had never sought to avail themselves of one, in the belief that their beloved country was the most beautiful in the world, so why look further? Vincenzo had to agree and had no real desire to venture into pastures new himself. Verdi was a good choice, unmarried and could be useful in the arrest of Kate Marshall, if they did, indeed, find her and Luca Buscolli.

"Make your arrangements, Verdi. We will leave tomorrow evening and meet with the Brite Agency boss, Jasmine Brite, and sort out our plan of action together. No hasty moves, this needs to be handled swiftly but delicately if we are to achieve anything. Of course, this might all be a wild goose chase and mere wishful thinking on my part - excuse my clichés - if I am wrong in my suspicions."

"Fine Sir, I will be ready to go with you tomorrow evening then."

Verdi, hid a look of relief from Vincenzo by turning and leaving the room quickly. *All is not lost, if I stay one step ahead and find Kate, if she is to be found at all, before anyone else, this disaster can be rectified*, thought Verdi, desperately. *It has to be.* Thank God, or more truthfully friends in low places, for a new identity, new passport, new Consulato Onorario d'Italia, new identity. *Nothing will be allowed to take this away from me, for something I did so long ago and through no fault of my own, I will see to that, for sure.*

44
The Brite Missing Persons Agency, England

RAPELLI and Verdi had arrived at Heathrow Airport the evening before and had stayed in a hotel close to the airport overnight. They had enjoyed a leisurely breakfast then continued their journey. Jasmine had given them instructions to catch a train to her home town, where she would meet them off the train. She had convinced them that this was the quickest and easiest way to travel from London.

Early afternoon found all three entering the offices of the Brite Agency, and Jasmine quickly introduced the two Italians to the rest of her team. Verdi remained in the background and left the talking to the boss.

Jasmine and Vincenzo stayed locked in conversation in her office for a long time, constructing a plan that would either come to nothing if the lead proved worthless, or would set in motion an international court case. Each step was vital and had to be conducted within legal constraints, to ensure the result was a trial of Kate Marshall and anyone who had helped her commit the crime of kidnapping Luca Buscolli.

Vincenzo was now convinced Kate had been party to the original kidnapping but Jasmine was less sure. The truth was she didn't want to believe it. It was too awful and whatever the outcome she was dreading having to contact Santa Buscolli with the results of the investigation. Of course, her greatest wish was that the two were still alive and well, but that would throw up a whole different set of problems for Santa. This would be worldwide news and a certain prison sentence for Kate. A little bit of her hoped that they were mistaken in her having travelled to England in 1978, and having lived a lie for thirty years. And what of Luca? Taken away from his family and denied a life of wealth and his Italian heritage. They must find out the truth of it all and as soon as possible. Jasmine hoped that Kate had been a victim too, rather than a criminal, just a kid and in terrible trouble, a teenager alone in a foreign country. She could not imagine what had been going on in her mind if the latter was true.

The plan, Jasmine and Vincenzo decided, was to go early the next morning to Maggie Tunstall's farm in Cumbria, arriving unexpectedly, giving no one the chance to escape, if they were there.

They explained the plan to the rest of her team and Verdi which set up an air of high anticipation and excitement that they might be about to solve a high-profile crime. It would certainly be good for the Brite business; yet most of them could not quite believe that an eighteen-year-old girl, could have pulled the whole thing off.

Jasmine explained that she and Evie would go as one team to supposedly interview Maggie Tunstall in person, and Vincenzo and Sergeant Verdi would follow behind, waiting nearby in an official capacity to arrest Kate and her aunt formally, then to inform the British authorities forthwith, if Kate and Luca proved to be at the farm, as they hoped.

They all planned to go out for a meal, aiming to be home early with the two Italian officers back at their hotel in the town to get a good night's rest before setting out for what might be a monumental day. Before leaving the hotel, Rappelli asked the receptionist to organise a hire car to be available as early as possible in the morning, charging it to himself. He would claim expenses later, if this investigation became active. Otherwise he would have to pick up the cost himself, or charge it to Santa Buscolli which he didn't really want to do but she had instigated the search, after all.

Verdi, on the other hand, had a different itinerary, having decided to telephone the car hire company to request a change of time for the car, to have it at the hotel that evening. It was vital to get to Kate, if she was with her aunt, before all hell broke loose and to convince her to run, for both their sakes.

Vincenzo woke up at 7.30 a.m. to find that Verdi had placed a note under his hotel room door informing him that the hire car had been used to travel to Birmingham Airport, as a death in the family had meant an urgent return to Italy and sincere apologies for the inconvenience but it was an emergency.

Vincenzo roared in anger. *What the hell was Verdi thinking?* Just slinking off like that. He would have to phone Jasmine immediately and ask for her brother Hugo to accompany him to the farm as one officer might not be enough for the situation. Hugo would have to provide back-up if things got nasty. Vincenzo was very angry and Verdi would feel that anger as soon as they returned to Milan.

After inflicting his bad mood on Jasmine, she told Vincenzo to calm down and proceed as planned. She would see him outside the hotel in an hour and Hugo would drive.

This was it, the Buscolli case was about to break wide open or be put to rest, finally, as no more leads were ever likely to be forthcoming.

45

MEANWHILE, Verdi had reached Maggie Tunstall's farm. Ispettore Rappelli had requested that the satnav in the hire car be programmed in Italian so it had been easy to get onto the motorway and drive in the fast lane for most of the journey. It was 4 a.m., not quite daylight yet. From an elevated position on high ground Verdi could see lights on in the farmhouse. *Now*, thought Verdi, *how to proceed? Who was at the farm? Was Kate even there at all? If she was, would she recognise someone from thirty years ago? What would she look like, would she be recognisable? Would Luca be there too, a grown man?* All these questions swirled around in the Verdi's panicked head. So long ago, whole different lives led by all of them, only to be destroyed now for a crime committed in the flush of idealistic youth. *It is so unfair*, thought Verdi. *It will not all be destroyed, not if I can help it. I have worked all my life to make up for my part, which was so little, in the crime by becoming a police officer, who did only good and helped solve crimes not committed them. I do not deserve it all to be taken away by a stupid girl that made things ten times worse. Please God, let her not be there, let this all be a mistake, for all our sakes.*

Verdi waited as long as possible to move but bearing in mind, that the others would be on their way as soon as they had awoken. They would not waste any time. The backdoor of the farm had been open and shut frequently but it was impossible to make out who was doing the two and froing. There was livestock in the barns, by the sound of distant animal noises and a few sheep were scattered along the hillside. Were there cattle in the barns in need of milking? Maybe. The only thing to be done was to drive down the lane, knock on the door of the farmhouse and ask for directions or something if the person that answered was Maggie Tunstall or anyone else except Kate Marshall. If it was Kate, well who knew what questions would be uttered by either of them?

Anyway the arrival of a car to the isolated farm would bring someone to the door straightaway. Verdi parked at the end of the lane and walked over into the front yard. Immediately, a dog started barking from inside making knocking loudly on the door largely unnecessary. *This is the moment of truth*, thought Verdi, nervously.

A few moments went by, but it felt like an eternity to Verdi. Then, the door opened and the woman behind it shushed the dog at her heels and the smile on her face turned to one of puzzlement and then disbelief. She went to slam the door but Verdi but a foot in it. They had recognised each other almost immediately, it seemed, even with the toil of the last thirty years etched on their faces.

"It's…not possible!" Kate stammered, non-plussed. "No. It can't be you. You, here, now, how is it possible?" Confusion, disbelief and fear etched themselves in turn on her face.

"But it is Kate. Believe your eyes but please, I am here to help you. Trust me, let me in. You have little time." Verdi implored the frightened woman.

"Stefana! How can it be you and yet I know it is? I couldn't forget any of your faces. They are in my worst nightmares. I do not understand how you are here? You must go away from here. Oh God help us, what's happened?"

Stefana, alias Gianna Verdi, pushed against the door and this time Kate gave no resistance. They were in a large, warm farmhouse kitchen that was disarrayed with the everyday morning activity. Clothes drying by the open fire, kettle on the Aga cooker, pots and frying pans wafting out tantalising smells to Stefana, who had not eaten since yesterday evening.

"Sit and I will tell you. I am now Sergeant Gianna Verdi of the Milanese police here to find you and arrest you," she said sternly. It was vital to keep control of the situation. Kate was alone in the kitchen but Stefana needed to know who else was here with her on the farm. "Who is here with you?" she asked, sharply.

"I'm not alone. You need to leave," Kate demanded. She had lost her immediate fear.

"On the contrary, you need to leave immediately. My Ispettore and members of a missing person agency that your mother and aunt are already aware of and I suspect you too, are already on their way here. I have managed to get here before them to warn you that your crime of the abduction of Luca and escape, has been uncovered. Please believe me that I am here to help you and of course myself. If they find you here they will also discover my part in it all, unless I silence you, maybe? I suggest you do not want that to happen so I am offering you a choice. Once again, who is here with you? Luca? Your Aunt? Quickly, before it is too late for you."

Kate stared at the woman she had last seen in a dirty warehouse where she had been kept captive for days with her tiny charge and a woman had been killed. It was true that Davido Romano and Stefana, whatever her other name was, certainly not the one she was now using, had been the only ones in the gang that had treated Luca and herself with any kindness, but she was still a kidnapper and here she was again threatening her. Could she convince this woman that she was alone, and then what? She decided she had to hear what Stefana had to say. "Look, I'm all alone. My aunt is in the cowshed and Callum, Cal, who you know as Luca is up in the field behind the farmhouse working. We start the day early here and yes Luca has always been safe here with me. I'm his mother, as far as he knows." There was both sadness and guilt in her voice. "Please explain how they found me when they couldn't do so thirty years ago. Of course, I've always known that one day there would be a knock on the door, like today. A crime so terrible wouldn't go unpunished. I'm ready to be judged. I'm tired of the guilt that has broken my heart but most of all the fear that my beloved Cal would one day hear the awful truth about his mother. Me, not Francesca Buscolli. I've loved him since the moment I met him and will always do so. I did what I thought was best when I was still so young and my loving family protected me and my secret. We have suffered for our lies but I was too cowardly to tell Cal of his past for fear that he'd hate me. Of course, he will, why wouldn't he? What I did was the same as what you all did to us, but it was out of misplaced love on my part and not for money. I am ready to answer to your Ispettore and his colleagues, arrest me."

"What do you mean? You stupid woman, ready? I am not ready!" shouted Stefana, harshly. "We must go get your aunt and tell her what's happened. She must answer the door and convince Ispettore Rappelli that she lives here alone. Hide as much of your belongings as possible, quickly. He is here unofficially at the moment, just helping the agency with their case so he cannot enter the premises if not invited. Your aunt is a clever woman to have kept you and Luca so successfully hidden for all this time, so I am sure she can play her part easily. Then you must convince Luca to hide out with us until they are gone. Then we can all go about our lives as before. Why suffer needlessly. No one need judge us at all. We did what we had to do."

"No! I won't. It's over Stefana, over!" Kate shouted, in desperation.

Stefana reached over to Kate and grabbed her arm roughly and the dog growled menacingly.

"Get rid of that animal. Now!" screamed Stefana. "Or I will get rid of it for you!"

Kate soothed the dog and shut him outside in the backyard, Stefana still held tight to Kate's arm to prevent her doing anything stupid, like running.

As they turned back from the door, a sleepy little voice, filled with confusion, called out "Nanna?" A child stood at the top of the stairs leading to the second floor.

Kate gasped and put her hand over her mouth. Oh, God no, they had awakened the grandson she had hoped to have kept hidden from Stefana. *What now?* She thought, hopelessly.

Stefana gazed at the child and her mind worked rapidly, "Luca's child?" she asked, in wonder as the image of the child Luca flashed before her. This child could be no other than the offspring of that little boy of long ago.

"Go back up to bed, my love," Kate coaxed, quietly. "It is too early to get up and I'm sorry we woke you up. This is an old friend of Nanna's; we were just talking too loudly. Please up to bed now."

"I'm not tired now. Can I go and wake Auntie up? I'm hungry." The little boy wasn't interested in being cooperative and carried on down the stairs.

"Auntie is in bed? Who else is upstairs, little one? asked Stefana, smiling at the child.

"Nobody. Mummy and Daddy are outside with the cows, aren't they, Nanna?"

Kate let out a groan of anguish as a smile spread across Stefana's face. "So, Kate, you are not being as truthful as I would like. That is a big mistake."

"Please, Stefana let us solve this between us. Don't involve my family. I will listen to what you have to say, I promise. Let my grandson return to his bed and we will talk calmly."

"What, and give the rest of your family a chance to intervene, maybe? No Kate, it is too late for that. You must do as I say now. There is no time for your reasons not to help me. Do you know how they found you? They recovered a statement from Davido Romaro even when I had so carefully gotten rid of the original stored at my station, with great risk, to protect us all, Kate. In it my extremely vigilant Ispettore noticed that Davido had family in Genova, Genoa as you English say. This gave a spark to his imagination that led him to your escape. Do you know what happened to my love, Davido? I will tell you. My love could not live with the fact that you took Luca and did not let him return him to his family, as he would have done if you had only trusted him. But no Kate, you took Luca for your own reasons and destroyed Davido and my future with him too. You are responsible for him committing suicide, a crime against God. He can never rest in peace all because of you. You owe it to me to hide and let this be over. It is but a small thing to ask, do you not think?"

Kate stared at Stefana in horror. *Davido killed himself because of me?* Would the impact of her crime never end? Jacob had come further into the kitchen and was now approaching the kitchen table ready to sit and eat. Stefana immediately sat down next him, making it clear to Kate that she was not going to let the child go anywhere.

"Nanna, call Auntie and we can all sit down and have breakfast early," Stefana asked Kate, with a cold smile.

Kate was trapped. Stefana was making her intentions clear; *do as I say or things could get worse.* A child was involved now so what she did next affected him too. Would Stefana take Jacob captive to force her to cooperate? *Yes,* was the likely answer. She stood up and went to the bottom of the stairs and called her aunt, loudly.

After what seemed an eternity, Aunt Maggie appeared at the top of the stairs and came down, chuntering to herself. About to ask what the hell was up, she stopped mid-speech when she saw the stranger sitting next to Jacob, buttering a piece of bread for him, in a weird semblance of perfect domesticity.

She looked to Kate to explain.

"It's come, Auntie, I'm sorry. This is Stefana whom I last saw in Milan in 1978 and she has found us at last, along with the Milanese police. Please come and join us while she explains what she wants." Kate was speaking quietly so that Jacob did not sense the tension in the room.

Maggie did as she was told and sat on the other side of Jacob, anxious to try and separate him from the intruder. Whatever this woman from the past had come for, it would not be good. She knew that instinctively. This was the culmination of years of worry and deceit, she realised.

"I congratulate you in having given Kate and Luca a whole new life after such tragic circumstances, at great cost to yourself I suspect. I know only too well how such malignant secrets fester in the mind and body, even if kept hidden out of love. Sadly, my love was not enough for the man who saved your niece from a prison cell and retribution for her crime. I, in turn, have not had such a good life but I have worked hard to improve my English as you can see, it is always a good skill to have in the police force as is the obtaining of a passport. These things can be very useful in standing out amongst the more unadventurous of my colleagues, but I always feared that this case would come back to haunt me. It was the easiest thing to do to put myself forward to look for your Kate." Stefana addressed Maggie, still helping Jacob with his breakfast and maintaining contact with the child, giving Maggie a subtle warning not to do anything stupid. The appearance of a child had been a Godsend for her. She now had bargaining power to make Kate do as she was told.

"Yes, I helped Kate out of love and the realisation that she was trapped by you and your gang of murderous villains. She made a huge mistake and we have done everything to right that. Callum has had a good life, he is very happy and content and as you see has his own son and a partner. Please, please go and leave us be. I do not understand why you have come alone?" Maggie was puzzled.

"I would like nothing better than that and, indeed, that is why I am here. I came to warn Kate to run or hide whilst Ispettore Rappelli and the missing persons people arrive here. Which will be soon. I have managed to come ahead of them. All that was needed was for you to see them and make them believe you are here alone and that Kate and Luca were never here. I wish to take them away for a while until the investigators leave. Then we can all get on with our lives. Ispettore Rappelli is not here officially. It is just an idea they came up with between them. Helped by Kate's mother and you acting suspiciously, it seems from what I could gather from my boss. Now you must convince your niece to do as I ask."

"But, of course she will. It's an excellent idea. I must apologise to you. Thank you for coming to warn us. Kate what are you thinking? We must get you away as quick as possible. We don't have much time and we are wasting it. Go and fetch Cal and Jenny from the cowshed and I'll get Jacob dressed and ready." Maggie got up from the table in readiness to make haste.

"No, Aunt," Kate replied, firmly. "No. I'm not going to run this time. It's over. I want peace even though Cal, Luca, will never forgive me and I don't deserve him to. I have been waiting thirty years for my crime to catch up with me and it has been thirty years of hell. I watched my little boy grow into a man and have a child of his own but my heart was heavy with the weight of what I'd taken from him. His identity. It is over I say."

Maggie looked at her niece in despair, knowing the implications of this decision for them all, but also understanding the burden she had been under all this time, as she had been too. But, she had to convince Kate that this was not the time to confess out of some misguided sense of guilt. Cal, Jenny and Jacob's life would be altered forever too with Kate's capture and punishment.

What happened next negated her need to say anything. Stefana stood up from the table and swiftly pulled Jacob up into her arms. He was too surprised by this action to protest and looked at Kate for a reaction, who stood up ready to confront Stefana.

"Sit down!" bellowed Stefana. "Do not do anything stupid! See, your aunt is being sensible. We can do this. Now all of us will go to this cowshed and join Luca and his partner, shall we?"

Kate and Maggie could do nothing but agree whilst Stefana had Jacob in her arms. Who knew what she would do now? She was a desperate woman and Kate was not cooperating voluntarily.

46

STEFANA was frustrated and increasingly panicked. Things weren't going as planned. Kate was refusing to cooperate, which she had not foreseen as it was in Kate's interest to do as she had asked. It was such a small thing considering how she had lived a lie for so long. What was wrong with the woman? They could have concocted some story to tell Luca between them, without revealing his real identity. Now, things could easily get out of control. There was only one of her against three adults. *If only I could have brought my gun into the country*, she thought. At least the child was bargaining material; they would not do anything stupid that would endanger him.

She needed a weapon and fortunately the kitchen had plenty of sharp knives. She had killed before; she could do it again, if it meant keeping the life she had worked so hard to create for herself.

Maggie was all for the plan to hide but how could she convince Kate now Luca would be involved and could she keep control of the situation with a grown man in the picture. She must be on guard at all times.

They crossed over the farm yard to the cowshed, Stefana still holding the child with the two women in front of her. She had shown them the carving knife she now held behind his back. As they entered the building they were greeted by the sound of the milking machines going about their business. Luca was at the furthest end of the shed and his partner was busy near the cows. As the door to the barn opened she looked up.

"Carol, Maggie, what's up?" she asked, surprised to see them. Then she saw Stefana holding her son behind them and cried out in alarm. "Carol?"

"Stay calm, Jenny this can be sorted. Don't do anything silly and Jacob will be safe," Kate replied, trying to keep the fear from her voice. She knew from experience that if Stefana was panicked she could be capable of anything, even murder. She was desperate to continue the life that she had created for herself.

For Kate, once Luca knew what she herself had done, her own life was irrelevant. He had yet to notice their arrival, as the noise of the machines was drowning out their voices. Stefana told Kate to go over and bring him to them, but make him aware of the knife and how much danger his son was in.

"Cal!" shouted Kate as she reached the end of the cowshed.

He looked up, startled. "Hi, mum. What's up?" Then his attention was caught by the group at the other end of the shed. "What's going on. Who is that woman? Has there been an accident or something, you're all looking so scared? Why is Jacob up? Mum?"

"Please, Cal, don't make any sudden moves. Just come over with me and all will be explained. That woman is from my past and is dangerous. She is threatening Jacob so we must all do as she says. She has a knife and believe me she is capable of using it. She's desperate. I am so sorry to have brought this all down onto you all. You will never forgive me and I don't deserve to be."

Cal was speechless as he looked at his mother, uncomprehending anything she had just said, apart from the point that his son was in danger. He went to spring to the boy's defence but Kate grabbed his arm.

"Please Cal, keep calm. She will hurt him if you don't. She is in control."

He looked again at her and slowed down his pace and walked alongside her.

"Ah, Luca. So good to see you after so long although you do not remember me, of course. It is not good to see you or Kate really. I hoped never to see you both again but here we are. I am eager to get away and you will help me."

"Who is this, mum? What is she talking about? Luca, Kate? She has the wrong people, obviously" said Luca, understandably even more confused.

"Your mother, Kate, has a lot of explaining to do when we have time but you and your family and I need to take a journey away from this farm as quickly as possible before time runs out. Do as I say and your son will be safe. Try anything stupid and you will be sorry." Stefana said, coldly.

She put the wriggling child down to the floor but held on tight to his hand. Jacob wanted to go to his daddy but she refused to let go and he began to cry. "Shut this child up!" she shouted, angrily. She needed to be able to keep control of them all.

"Give him to me then, and I promise I'll stay by your side" begged Jenny. She looked imploringly at Luca. Please don't react badly, she silently pleaded with him. Without the knife and the threat to Jacob, and indeed them all, Cal could easily have overcome the woman and she didn't want him to try any heroics. First, they needed to know who she was and what she was doing here? It was to do with Carol, that's all she knew.

"We will all go back to the farmhouse and plan our next move. You!" She indicated Jenny. "Take the child's other hand and stay with me. You others go ahead and don't try anything."

They did as she said, walking in a line with Luca at the head. When they were back in the kitchen Stefana instructed them all to sit down, except for Jenny and Jacob who she ordered to go upstairs and dress the child for going out. She had taken the precaution of searching Jenny for a mobile phone, just in case she had any ideas and, once again, threatened them all with the fact that she had nothing to lose, if they did not do exactly as she asked. When Jenny had taken the boy upstairs, she spoke to Maggie. "You, I think see the plan clearly and know it is the sensible thing to do to convince Kate and Luca."

Once again, Luca asked in confusion. "Why does she keep calling us that?"

"Because that is who you are, my love," whispered Aunt Maggie.

Luca looked at his mother in astonishment. "What! I don't understand. What the hell is going on?"

"You are not the son of Kate Marshall, alias Carol Tunstall. You are Luca Buscolli, kidnapped, once in your home of Milano, Italy in 1978 and again by this woman months later and brought here. You must ask her why because I do not know why. She says out of love for you. You are about to be discovered, so if you want to continue this life with this woman, you must come with me and let your Aunt Maggie convince the police and English detectives that she lives alone. Then they will go away and nothing more will happen. Except, of course, Kate will have to face your judgement but not a prison sentence, if you do indeed forgive her. That is up to you," Stefana informed him, callously.

Kate's head was in her hands as Luca's looked for a denial from her. *A mistake surely? All a mistake, it has to be*, his expression said.

"Please change your mind, Carol and hide. Don't do this to us all. We have had a good life here, surely you know that. You are Carol, he is Callum. You risk us all going to prison because we helped you. Please!" begged Maggie.

"But don't you realise, Aunt? I want to be Kate whatever that brings with it. It has been a life sentence for me, that has got harder as Luca's grown up. Don't you realise how guilty I felt when he married Jenny and when Jacob was born? I have denied Luca and Jacob their birth right to part of the Buscolli dynasty, a rich and influential family. I denied that family a son and heir. I have been dreading this day coming for thirty years but I feel as though a great weight has been lifted from my shoulders and in my heart. No more, I say. I will not co-operate."

"You will!" Stefana bellowed, banging her fists on the table. She went to the stairs and shouted to Jenny to bring Jacob down and join them. "We will all go to my car, now." As Jacob reached the bottom step she scooped him up in her arms, despite his struggle to be let down, and held the knife pointing towards his neck.

He started to cry.

"Tell this child to shut up or else!," she instructed Jenny.

Terrified at the sight of the knife and of Stefana's volatile state, Jenny stroked her son's face and did her best to soothe him.

"Please, let me hold him. I will not do anything to prevent what you want us to do. Please for God's sake have some pity, he's an innocent child. Don't make the same mistakes again. We will co-operate, whatever Carol says."

"See that you do. Luca take hold of Kate and lead us all to the car," Stefana did as asked and returned the child to its mother.

"Do I come too?" asked Maggie.

"Yes. We will work out what you will say when they arrive, which will be only too soon I fear. We must hurry to get some distance away until they have gone. I will take us on a little drive." She gestured to Luca to lead Kate, with Maggie behind them and then Jenny carrying Jacob, whilst she still held the knife behind Jacob's back so that he could not see it, but they all knew it was there.

They reached the car and Stefana shut Jenny and Jacob in the back and instructed Luca to sit in the front seat. Then she locked the doors.

She was left with Kate and Maggie to plan what would happen next. She said that she would only take them along the country lanes and park up in a wooded area, of which there were many in this secluded area. She thanked God that Maggie's farm was so isolated, with no nosey neighbours to worry about. Of course, this had suited the family well in hiding of Kate and Luca from the world.

Meanwhile Stephana's plan was that Maggie would continue the milking of the cows and go about her daily duties as if nothing had happened. When Ispettore Rappelli and the Brite agency people arrived, she should be in the kitchen as usual and invite them in. Maggie would have hidden all evidence of family living from the room and she would inform them that she lived alone with help from a couple of locals who came when needed. She would once again deny all knowledge of what had happened to her niece in 1978 and state that she had only seemed angered at their questions before, because she had been worried what the effect would be on her sister's mental health of dragging old memories up again. Her sister had made peace with the fact that her daughter was dead and had learned to live with it, as had they all, she would tell them.

Hopefully, satisfied that they had jumped to the wrong conclusions the detectives would take their leave and the case would be wound up. Stefana could return to Milan and the Tunstalls could carry on with their lives as before. Maggie would be able to placate Kate and, together, the two of them would find a way to tell Luca that they had kept him out of love not criminality. "Hopefully," she said again.

Kate remained silent and the two women, having no idea whether she was agreeing to the plan or not, decided this was for the best.

Stefana gave Maggie her phone number and told her to phone when it was over and she was alone again. She trusted Maggie not to phone anyone as soon as the car had gone, for she knew it would be foolish to sacrifice her own life when they could get away with it again. Stefana opened the backdoor of the car and told Jenny to get out and sit in the front beside Luca. Then she put Jacob on Kate's lap as she got in beside her in the back. She held the knife close to Kate's ribs and Jacob's chest and made sure Luca could see them in the rear-view mirror. One false move and she would use it, her eyes were telling him. She handed him the car keys and they drove off slowly, out of the farmyard, along the steep lane and off in the countryside in search of a secluded spot to lay low.

Luca obviously knew the area backwards but Stefana warned him not to be stupid and try to take them somewhere that they could be rescued. It was in Kate's interest not to be found. Arrest Stefana, arrest Kate and Maggie too. Not an option. She hoped he loved them as much as they loved him. He calmly replied that he had no intention of endangering his family and drove on.

They went on for half an hour or so, when suddenly Kate seemed to awaken from a shocked stupor and said, "I'm not doing it Stefana. As soon as you go from here, I'll alert the police. I don't care what you say. Let my family go and we can end this together. I will not tell them about you but I will confess."

"Confess! Confess to who? You will be dragged back to Milan and put in a cell. All you feared thirty years ago. You have no proof you were innocent. They will beat my name out of you, learn of Carla, everything you stupid, stupid woman. I came here to help. Why can you not understand?" Stefana was almost screaming with frustration.

"I want to be punished for taking Luca away from his family, for letting him get kidnapped in the first place. I will have some kind of peace. Why can't you understand? Go now and save yourself. Disappear again somewhere in Italy. Just don't ask me again to live this lie."

"Stupido!" Stefana, in fury struck Kate hard across the face.

Jacob cried out, as he fell sideways as the blow rocked his putative grandmother. "Leave my Nanna alone. Daddy, see what she did?" With that he balled his little fists up and went to strike Stefana.

She caught his arm and instinctively hit him too, out of control now. Suddenly, Luca let out a cry of pure animalistic rage, hit the brakes, seat belt pinging back as he swung over the front seat and punched Stefana squarely on the chin. It stunned her but she instantly flayed about with the knife, lashing out at him, catching him on his forearm, making the blood splash over Jacob who was now screaming in terror.

Kate grabbed Stefana's arm, attempting to twist the knife out of her hand, even as she continued to lash out at Luca. He was bleeding profusely but threw another punch into Stefana's face, slowing her down and finally giving Kate the opportunity to snatch the knife away, albeit by the blade. Her hand spurted blood from the cut but she had the weapon now.

Jacob was hysterical, caught in the middle of the fight, but Kate pushed him down onto the car floor and helped Luca make one last huge joint effort to overcome Stefana. The defeated woman was straddled by Kate and Luca struck the final blow that knocked her out cold.

Here in Britain and Italy, what came next would be watched by an eager audience, fed by a media only too ready to report melodrama, without reflecting on the human sacrifice it incurred.

THE AFTERMATH

THE world did, indeed, go crazy for the sensational story of the little Italian boy who was kidnapped by his nanny and turned up on an isolated farm in Cumbria, thirty years later. The full story was kept for the courts in England and Italy with long drawn out trials for all involved. News stories involve real lives, with all the emotion and heartbreak that a jury has to consider, whilst coming to the correct decision, an unenviable task but necessary.

On that fateful day when the accused found their quiet, ordinary lives, come crashing down around their ears the local police had walked into a scene more in keeping with a TV crime show than the quiet, rural community the Cumbrian constabulary were used to, but they stepped up to the mark after the details were explained by the Italian policeman, Ispettore Rappelli.

They re-arrested the suspects, to satisfy English jurisdiction. They were unfamiliar with cross-country protocol, having never come across it before in their careers as rural policemen but others could handle all that later when the cases were passed on to higher levels along with the Italian authorities and a trial set.

Jasmine and the Brite Agency played a vital role in presenting evidence for the trial along with Vincent and Enzo Rappelli and as a result, found themselves achieving a notoriety which resulted in them being inundated with missing person cases, a fact that would be financially beneficial to the agency in future years. They couldn't have asked for better publicity than this high-profile case, after all, and yet, it was with sadness that this bonus was looked upon by all involved.

Even though they had found living souls not corpses, the result had not been a happy one, with the reunion of the lost and their elated families.

For Santa Buscolli, who had instigated the search for her little brother, and Luca Buscolli, the reunion was a painful meeting between two strangers, with Santa realising that she was still alone even after finding Luca, and questioning whether she should have left well alone, considering the consequences to him and all involved.

Their meeting was arranged by Jasmine after she had explained everything that had happened to Santa, who had rewarded the Brite Agency with a generous fee.

Max, the lawyer and friend to both women, had accompanied Jasmine to offer advice and comfort to Santa. The shock had been great for her as she learnt of Luca's true parentage and how closely he had been living to her, a mere journey up to the North, for all these years. If only her mother had continued to search for him, but perhaps, she lacked the will. He was not her child at all and she had never acted as a mother really. Kate had taken over that role.

So, whilst Kate languished in prison on remand and June and Maggie were out on bail, awaiting trial, Santa and Luca got to tell each other their stories and to try to make sense of it all.

Luca insisted on being called Cal, just as he had always had been, as far as he had known and sadly, they could not find any common ground to unite them. Santa was Italian and Luca considered himself English, having no memory of his life before coming to Cumbria. It took him many months of counselling and frequent trips to visit Kate in prison, whom he still called Mum, to come to terms with what she had done, but his love for her over-ruled everything else and he had begged Santa to help his mother by forgiving the teenager forced to make adult decisions, just as he had forgiven her. He stressed it would not change things; what was done was done, but the judge might be more lenient if the victims of her crime could forgive her, or seem to, at least.

Santa did not want to cause Luca more anguish so she agreed to give a statement asking for leniency, but she could not find it in her heart to forgive. For her, Kate had robbed her family of a son and brother; maybe not a true one but no one would have known that, and her life had always had the shadow of the terrible loss of Luca hanging over her. No, she could not forgive. However, she arranged through Max, to transfer a substantial amount of her inheritance to be paid to Luca. He said he would use a large amount of it to employ Max as Kate's lawyer and Santa had to accept his loyalty. He had not wanted to take any of the inheritance, unless he could use it this way and as there would still be plenty left he promised that it would be put in a Trust Fund for Jacob, who was a legitimate member of the Buscolli dynasty, albeit not the grandson of Marcello and Francesca Buscolli but a second nephew.

Santa and Luca met a few times during the trial as they were witnesses for the defence and had to recount their stories under oath but they could not find any real connection as brother and sister and did not continue to try.

Finally, taking into account the circumstances of the original kidnapping in 1978, Kate's immaturity and her fear of the consequences from the Buscolli family and the Italian justice system - she had been told horror stories of people being slung into prison to rot away, wildly exaggerated it must be said, but harsher than English justice - Kate was sentenced to ten years for the concealment and abduction of a minor.

She would serve her sentence in England.

June Marshall and Margaret Tunstall were both given two-year suspended sentences, taking into account their ages and their emotional connection to Kate Marshall and their compulsion to protect her, for aiding and abetting a crime.

Stefana Verdi's trial took place in Milan many months later than Kate's, as the wheels of justice moved slower and the trial involved the original kidnapping and the subsequent murder of Carla Torello. Her body had been recovered from the deep hole after Stefana had admitted everything and shown them where it was hidden.

Ispettore Rappelli was in charge of gathering all the evidence for trial, calling upon the relevant witnesses, those who were still alive, and getting the case ready for trial. Stefana after many months in Jail was a broken woman and admitted her part in the kidnapping and accidental death of Carla. She was tried in the Milanese courts and sentenced to life for the kidnapping of Luca and Kate, the second degree murder of Carla and obtaining a false identity, to be served in the notoriously harsh San Vittore prison in the centre of Milan.

Ispettore Rappelli was satisfied that at last justice for Luca had been done and the case was closed for good. Jasmine had given evidence throughout the trial of her part in the discovery of evidence and had stayed with the Rappellis, as her relationship with Enzo was still very much ongoing.

Santa had also journeyed to Milan for the trial. The press had been full of the sensational crime. Once again, witnesses sold their stories, including Lynne Rossi after being forced to tell her husband of her connection, as Kate's friend.

Eventually though, it was over and the press lost interest and moved on to other news. Life got back to normal for everyone involved, except for the accused.

Vincent and Enzo returned to their daily life solving crime and controlling traffic. They had both received commendations for their part in solving the crime and Enzo was assured he would not be long in progressing from traffic control to crime solving, within his father's team.

As for Luca Buscolli, who continued to call himself Callum Tunstall, this time legally by deed poll, he returned to the farm with Jenny, Jacob and Aunt Maggie and continued the life he had always known and wanted. The only element missing in the picture was his mother.

EPILOGUE
2016 HM Prison Low Newton, County Durham

THE summer sun was beating down on the car roof, making the interior stifling and airless, even with the window open. England was basking in a glorious heatwave. The atmosphere was close and full of nervous energy.

Cal sat tapping his fingers on the steering wheel, anxious to get moving but with no choice but to wait.

Finally, the surprisingly small outer door to the prison opened and out stepped a frail looking, grey-haired woman, who seemed to blink in the bright sun and look around bewildered, as if she could not believe she was out, on the other side of walls that had held her for eight long years.

She had been given two years off her sentence for good behaviour.

As she stood there, Cal got out of the car and made his way over to Kate. He embraced her and planted a kiss on her forehead before saying, "Come on Mum, let's go home."

FICTION FROM APS BOOKS
(www.andrewsparke.com)

Davey J Ashfield: *Footsteps On The Teign*
Davey J Ashfield *Contracting With The Devil*
Davey J Ashfield: *A Turkey And One More Easter Egg*
Davey J Ashfield: *Relentless Misery*
Fenella Bass: *Hornbeams*
Fenella Bass:: *Shadows*
Fenella Bass: *Darkness*
HR Beasley: *Nothing Left To Hide*
Lee Benson: *So You Want To Own An Art Gallery*
Lee Benson: *Where's Your Art gallery Now?*
Lee Benson: *Now You're The Artist...Deal With It*
Lee Benson: *No Naked Walls*
TF Byrne *Damage Limitation*
Nargis Darby: *A Different Shade Of Love*
J.W.Darcy *Looking For Luca*
J.W.Darcy: *Ladybird Ladybird*
J.W.Darcy: *Legacy Of Lies*
J.W.Darcy: *Love Lust & Needful Things*
Paul Dickinson: *Franzi The Hero*
Jane Evans: *The Third Bridge*
Simon Falshaw: *The Stone*
Milton Godfrey: *The Danger In Being Afraid*
Chris Grayling: *A Week Is...A Long Time*
Jean Harvey: *Pandemic*
Michel Henri: *Mister Penny Whistle*
Michel Henri: *The Death Of The Duchess Of Grasmere*
Michel Henri: *Abducted By Faerie*
Laurie Hornsby: *Postcards From The Seaside*
Hugh Lupus *An Extra Knot (Parts I-VI)*
Alison Manning: *World Without Endless Sheep*
Ian Meacheam: *An Inspector Called*
Ian Meacheam: *Time And The Consequences*
Ian Meacheam: *Broad Lines Narrow Margins*
Alex O'Connor: *Time For The Polka Dot*
Mark Peckett: *Joffie's Mark*
Peter Raposo: *dUst*

APS PUBLICATIONS

Printed in Great Britain
by Amazon

85996996R00115